For Your Love

Book 2

Loving You Series

by

Vanessa Miller

For Your Love

Vanessa Miller

Book 2
Loving You Series

Publisher's Note:

This short story is a work of fiction. References to real events, organizations, or places are used in a fictional context. Any resemblances to actual persons, living or dead are entirely coincidental.

Vanessa Miller

www.vanessamiller.com

Printed in the United States of America
© 2019 by Vanessa Miller

Praise Unlimited Enterprises
Charlotte, NC

Other Books by Vanessa Miller

Family Business I
Family Business II
Family Business III
Family Business IV
Family Business V
Family Business VI
Our Love
For Your Love
Got To Be Love
Rain in the Promised Land
Heaven Sent
Sunshine And Rain
After the Rain
How Sweet The Sound
Heirs of Rebellion
Feels Like Heaven
Heaven on Earth
The Best of All
Better for Us
Her Good Thing
Long Time Coming
A Promise of Forever Love
A Love for Tomorrow
Yesterday's Promise
Forgotten
Forgiven
Forsaken
Rain for Christmas (Novella)

Through the Storm
Rain Storm
Latter Rain
Abundant Rain
Former Rain

Anthologies (Editor)
Keeping the Faith
Have A Little Faith
This Far by Faith

Novella

Love Isn't Enough
A Mighty Love
The Blessed One (Blessed and Highly Favored series)
The Wild One (Blessed and Highly Favored Series)
The Preacher's Choice (Blessed and Highly Favored Series)
The Politician's Wife (Blessed and Highly Favored Series)
The Playboy's Redemption (Blessed and Highly Favored Series)
Tears Fall at Night (Praise Him Anyhow Series)
Joy Comes in the Morning (Praise Him Anyhow Series)
A Forever Kind of Love (Praise Him Anyhow Series)
Ramsey's Praise (Praise Him Anyhow Series)
Escape to Love (Praise Him Anyhow Series)
Praise For Christmas (Praise Him Anyhow Series)
His Love Walk (Praise Him Anyhow Series)
Could This Be Love (Praise Him Anyhow Series)
Song of Praise (Praise Him Anyhow Series)

Prologue

On a cold day in December, Toya Milner was at the hospital with her family. But this time, it was for a joyous occasion. Her younger sister, Tia, had just given birth to a baby girl, Jayden Trinity Carter. She was seven pounds and two ounces of pure beauty, even if she was still all wrinkly and reddish-brown.

Robbie sat on the edge of Tia's bed and held his little girl as if she were some rare, irreplaceable jewel that could break if mishandled. "She's so beautiful. I can't believe this is really our daughter," Robbie said with tears glistening in his eyes.

"Hey, speak for yourself," Tia said. "I am more than capable of making a beautiful child."

The room erupted in laughter. Toya's mother, Pastor Yvonne Milner, was standing next to her co-pastor and Toya's godfather, Thomas Reed. He put his hand on Yvonne's shoulder, and Toya smiled at the sight of them openly displaying affection for each other. They had weathered many storms in the past year, but with the help of the Lord, they had come through it all. Thomas had been patient with her as she'd grown more comfortable with accepting her love for him.

Toya sat in the rocking chair next to the window, waiting for a chance to hold her niece. She smiled at her family, but in truth, Toya wondered when she would have what her mom and Thomas have, or even what Tia and Robbie have. She had been abused by love and wasn't trying to rush back out there, but still, there was something deep inside her that was longing for a love that was true.

Jarrod, Thomas' son, stood behind her. He had been the first man to break her heart, it was only a testament to the God she served that she was able to be friends with him again.

Jarrod poked her arm as he asked, "So if Auntie Yvonne is my godmother, does that make Jayden my god-niece, or what?"

"She could be just your niece if you'd pick up the speed and ask Toya out already," Tia chided him.

Seeing the embarrassed look on Jarrod's face, Yvonne retorted, "Hey, you leave Jarrod alone."

Yeah, leave Jarrod alone, Toya wanted to yell at her sister. The last thing she needed would be for Jarrod to ask her out and not show up again. No, thank you.

Robbie stood up and handed the baby to Toya, then turned back to Tia and cleared his throat. "Tia? I...uh, I'd like to be more to you than just your baby's daddy. I understand why you didn't marry me before, but I have changed. I've been on my job now for over three months and haven't missed a day or gotten written up or anything. I want to be a family. So, what I'm asking is, will you please marry me?"

Tia smiled but then hesitated. "That depends. Will you come to the wedding drunk again?"

"You know I haven't had a thing to drink in months. I'm a Christian now, Tia, and that means something to me. The Lord is helping me to stay sober."

"Well, all right then, Robbie Carter. I guess I'll marry you," Tia said.

The room erupted in cheers. Toya had secretly been rooting for Robbie ever since that night at the hospital when Robbie had refused to leave Tia's side. She'd seen then that the boy had grown into a man—a man well able to take care of his family.

"Okay, why don't we give them some privacy?" Thomas suggested.

After they'd said good-bye to the new parents and baby Jayden, Thomas, Yvonne, Jarrod, and Toya were all about to go to dinner, but Thomas stunned them all when he took hold of Yvonne's hand and slyly grinned. "Well, what about you, Yvonne? Do you think you'll ever marry me?"

"That depends," she said with a hint of mischief in her voice. "Are you going to come to the wedding drunk?"

"Drunk in the spirit and drunk in love? You bet," Thomas answered, then wrapped his arms around her and kissed her tenderly.

When he released her, Yvonne smiled. "Well, in that case, I guess I have no choice but to marry you."

"You always have a choice."

Yvonne shook her head. "I never had a choice, Thomas. You stole my heart, and I don't ever want it back."

"So, it's mine forever?"

"How about… as long as we both shall live?"

Toya glanced over at Jarrod while all this was going on. Her mom and her sister were getting married, but she couldn't seem to find a man… well, there were plenty of men around, but what she needed was a good man.

Jarrod nudged her. "You're next."

Why did he have to say that? She didn't want to hear that from anyone, and especially not the man who provided her with her first broken heart. And she really didn't want to talk about finding love when she was still getting over what happened with Marvel Williams. The man who tricked her into believing he was in love with her, then tried to kill her.

~~~

"Where is the money you promised me?" Clarence Brown asked his partner in crime.

"I don't pay for failed jobs."

"Speak for yourself, Marvel. Because I didn't fail at anything. I practically bankrupted my own church, all you had to do was convince the city to sell you the church. But you were the one who was more interested in destroying Pastor Yvonne and her daughter than making the deal you told me you wanted."

"That's neither here nor there, Brown. I still didn't get what I wanted. And unless you can find out where Toya is, I'm not giving you my money."

"But my wife needs that money. The only reason I got involved with you in the first place was to get her the heart operation she desperately needs."

"Then I suggest you get the information that I desperately need." Marvel hung up and then kicked the trash can next to his desk. Toya and her mother had ruined everything for him. There were warrants out for his arrest, he couldn't run his businesses, and he was stuck in Mexico. But his suffering was nothing compared to what Pastor Yvonne and Toya would soon feel. Revenge was always sweet.

1

Two weddings in the space of three months were almost more than Toya Milner could take, especially since she was a bridesmaid in both weddings. But she couldn't let her mother or sister down. So, Toya smiled her way through her mother's wedding because she was truly happy that her mother had found love again. Her father passed away over three years ago, and her mother had grieved long and hard. It was time for her to smile again.

But today, she was wearing a peach bridesmaid gown because it was her sister Tia's turn to get married. And Tia picked peach as her color even though pastels weren't a good look for Toya. Tia was marrying the father of her child, the man she truly loved. Robbie Carter turned out to be a good guy, and Toya was glad that they had each other. But the reason the smile she felt in her heart for her sister wasn't shining through her eyes today was simply that Toya wanted a love of her own and didn't understand why she couldn't meet a man who wasn't trying to use or abuse her.

"Hey, no frowning. This is a happy day," Jarrod Reed said as he put an arm around her shoulder and lightly nudged her.

"Of course, it's a happy day." Jarrod was way too close for her liking. Toya stepped back, letting his arm fall off her shoulder. "Where is your date? Why are you over here bothering me about my facial expressions?"

"Since you are now my sister, I think it is more than appropriate that I am concerned about you being a big ol' grump on the happiest day of our other sister's life."

Toya gave him the hand. "Just because your father married my mother, does not make us brother and sister."

"Why doesn't it?" Jarrod demanded to know.

"It just doesn't." Toya walked away from Jarrod because she couldn't explore all the reasons why being his sister didn't work for her. Maybe if he weren't so gorgeous, Toya wouldn't have fantasized about being his wife when they were teenagers. But none of that matters anymore, especially since Jarrod stood her up for her senior prom.

Her cell phone rang. She looked at the caller ID, but the number was private. She never answered private numbers, but for some reason, she hit the accept button.

As she was trying to say hello, she was interrupted, "I know it's not right to call you, but I need help."

A chill went down Toya's spine as she thought for just a moment that the caller sounded like Marvel Williams. "Why are you calling me? What do you want?"

"I'm not trying to cause no trouble, but I'm living on the street. I can't even feed myself. I just want you to talk to your mother for me. Tell her to let me come back home."

"Deacon Brown?" Toya couldn't believe the nerve of this man. He and Marvel had plotted against her mother, and now he wanted help.

"It's me. I called you because I know that you have a big enough heart to forgive a foolish old man. Like the prodigal son, I went out into the world and made a mess of my life. I now know how good I had it, and I want to come back to the church."

"You embezzled money from the church. Why on earth do you think my mother would just let you waltz back into Christ Life Sanctuary as if you didn't try to tear it down?"

"I wasn't thinking right back then. But tell your mom that I really need her help. My wife is sick. She needs a heart operation, but the church cut off my insurance, and I can't afford to pay for her operation."

Before Toya could respond, Jarrod snatched the phone away from her ear. "How dare you get Toya involved in this dumpster fire you created. Turn yourself into the police. Accept responsibility for what you did. Until you do that, we don't want to hear from you again." Jarrod hung up and handed the phone back to Toya.

"I was handling the situation myself. I didn't need you to come over here, like I'm some damsel in distress."

"Whether you like it or not, I'm going to always have your back." He got in her face and rubbed noses with her. "You're stuck with me so just face it."

"Whatever." Shaking her head, Toya put her cell back in her purse and headed for the door. All this family togetherness and wedding stuff was more than she could take. She needed to break free and get back to life as she knew it. But ever since that incident with Marvel, life just hadn't been the same.

In the space of a few hours, everything had changed for her. Now, as she walked out of the hotel where Tia's wedding reception was being held, she looked around, taking in every sight and sound before stepping out of the building. The day Marvel kidnapped her; Toya hadn't been aware of her surroundings as she left her office building.

He had been standing by the trunk of his car, smiling at her as if everything was still good between them, even though they both knew it wasn't. Even so, Toya never expected Marvel to pull a gun on her or to demand that she get in his car. The rest was all too painful to think about as she quickly got in her car and locked the doors. As she turned on the engine, Toya glanced around, checking her surroundings once again. That's when she noticed Jarrod standing a few feet away with his back against the concrete wall as if he thought he could blend in.

She rolled her window down and yelled so he could hear her, "It's daylight, Jarrod. I don't need a bodyguard right now."

"How do you know I'm not out here taking a smoke break?" He said as he walked over to her car.

Toya rolled her eyes. "Show me your smokes."

"Don't try to bum cigs off of me. You earn enough money at that law firm to buy your own."

"I'm on leave from my law firm, and you don't smoke."

Jarrod threw up his hands. "Okay, you've got me. I was following you. But you can't just be wandering off on your own like that." When he caught the look she gave him, he said, "Yeah, yeah, yeah, I know you're grown. But help a brother out. I've been defending you since we were kids. Remember that bully who wanted to fight you just because you wouldn't give him a kiss. Who took that beat down for you?"

Toya laughed at the memory. They had been in the sixth grade when Jarrod became her hero. The bully's nickname was Meathead because he had a fat head. But that wasn't all. His stomach hung over his pants, and he had arms like Terry Crews, the ex-football player, turned actor.

That bruiser landed one punch to Jarrod's cheek and knocked him on the ground. Toya and Tia then jumped on the bruiser's back and pounded on his head until the school security guard pulled them off. They all received a one-day suspension, but it was worth it because that big boy never bothered her again. "I don't want you to get beat up by Deacon Brown, so just stay out of it."

"Ha ha, very funny. But I think I can take Deacon Brown. It's you I'm worried about. I don't want you caught up in all that drama again, Toya. I'm serious about that."

Jarrod gave her that look. The one that told her he was about business and wasn't in the mood for games. "I'm not going to meet up with Deacon Brown. So, stop worrying."

Toya couldn't even be annoyed at Jarrod for watching out for her. He'd done that since they were kids. But as she drove home, she wondered why in the world he was still single. She and Jarrod would be turning thirty-two this year. So, it was time for that man to settle down. He would make a wonderful husband and father. Toya had thought about introducing Jarrod to one of her sorority sisters but had never followed through on that.

When she arrived home, Toya pulled up to her mailbox, rolled her window down, and took the mail out of the box. She opened the garage door, drove into her garage and quickly put the garage door back down all the while looking through her rearview mirror to ensure that no one tried to sneak into the garage.

Before opening the door to enter her home through the kitchen, Toya said a silent prayer asking God to protect her and make sure that no one was inside her house waiting to kill her. She entered the townhouse and turned off the alarm system. The fact that the alarm had not been set off was another way she ensured that no one evaded her home. Toya leaned against the wall next to the alarm and exhaled. This had become her ritual every time she had to re-enter her home.

Toya solved this problem by quitting her job at her law firm and only leaving the house when absolutely necessary. She knew this behavior wasn't normal and that she should probably see a therapist. But how would she explain that to her mother who thought that Jesus could solve every problem? Would her mother think less of her for needing something other than Jesus?

2

Two days later, while in her pajamas, Toya lounged in her living room, with her feet propped on her ottoman while she searched the internet for a job she could work from home. She had enough savings to get her through the next few months as she figured out her next move. But she definitely would have to figure out something because she was not some trust fund baby who could just live off the wealth others left behind.

Her mother and stepfather were well off, but that was their money. She was a big girl and had been taking care of herself since the day she left law school. As she tapped her fingers on the keyboard of her laptop, Toya wondered for the hundredth time if she needed to see someone about this fear that she had allowed to rule and reign in her life to the point of not even wanting to leave the house.

She clicked off the job site and opened a Google search. Just as Toya started typing in her search for a psychologist, she felt thirsty, so she went into the kitchen to get a drink of water. While there she noticed crumbs on the counter, that began her hour-long procrastination project. Because she didn't just wipe the crumbs off the counter, but then the stove needed to be cleaned, the floor had to be swept, and the microwave and fridge had to been wiped down.

Just when Toya was starting to feel guilty about procrastinating on finding a job and a psychologist to speak to, her phone rang. Glancing at the caller ID, she saw that it was Jarrod.

"Hey Bubba," Toya answered with the affectionate name she had given Jarrod when they were kids.

"How many times do I have to tell you not to call me that?"

"I don't say it in public. I think that's a good compromise, don't you?"

"Whatever. Where are you?"

"I'm at home. Why what's up?"

"We've got a problem. Deacon Brown just went live on Facebook."

"I don't see why that's our problem. I hope he provided his address while he was doing that live video so the police can finally arrest him."

"Do me a favor, Toya?"

"As long as I can do it in my PJs, you've got it."

"Get dressed. I'm on my way to get you… and don't go to Facebook until I've told you everything. Promise?"

Toya had no idea what Jarrod was all up in arms about. But she parted ways with her cleaning rag and closed the fridge. After jumping in the shower, she put on a pair of stonewashed jeans, a white tank top with a soft pink button-down knit sweater and a pair of clogs that were made of blue jean material. Just as she thought that she looked comfortable but cute, another thought struck.

Could she break out and run if need be in these clogs. Cute was one thing, but surviving an attack was another matter. The doorbell rang as she was searching for her Nikes. She let Jarrod in. "Just give me a minute. I'm searching for another pair of shoes."

"Oh no you don't. The shoes you have on are fine. We need to get going." Jarrod grabbed Toya's arm and pulled her toward the front door.

Toya snatched away. "I'm serious, Jarrod. What if something happens and we need to get away quickly. I'd never make it." She turned and headed back to her bedroom as if what she said made perfect sense.

Jarrod had been smiling as he playfully tried to pull Toya toward the door, but after seeing the look of fear on her face and her explanation for changing her shoes, he wasn't smiling anymore. As he walked into her bedroom and entered her walk-in closet, he told her. "Don't worry about the shoes, Toya. I'll go to the hospital myself."

Her closet was a mess. Dirty clothes piled high on one side and stacks of flies and paper on the other side. Her shoes were somewhere in the middle, she just needed to find them. "Hospital? Who's in the hospital?" Toya turned and fell back on the mound of dirty clothes.

Jarrod offered a hand. "Let me get you out of here before we won't be able to find you."

"Yeah, okay, very funny." Toya grabbed hold of Jarrod's hand and let him lift her up. As they walked back into the living room, she said, "My closet isn't normally like that. You just caught me on a bad day."

"Don't even start lying like that Toya. It looks like something exploded in your closet. That took more than a day."

"I'm not a slob, Jarrod. So, stop acting like I need to be on Hoarders."

"I know you're not a slob. You're usually very organized, with a place for everything, and everything in its place."

"Yes, but this townhouse is too small. I don't have any storage space, so it's hard to get everything organized."

"Why did you sell your condo anyway. I really liked that place."

Averting her eyes, she answered, "I didn't want to stay there anymore. And besides, this townhouse has a connected garage, and it's in a gated community with security. I like it. But you still haven't answered my question. Who is in the hospital? And why didn't you want me to go on Facebook?"

He sat down and pointed at the chair across from him, inviting her to do the same. "Deacon Brown is in the hospital. He shot himself on a Facebook Live video."

"What?" It felt like the air swooshed out of her body and forced her to sit down.

"I reported the video, so Facebook took it down, thank God. But the man is desperate."

"Desperate enough to kill himself?" Toya didn't know what to think or feel about this. Deacon Brown had reached out to her for help, and she had just ignored the man.

"Not only that. He shot himself in front of the police station. That was his way of turning himself in, I guess."

"Did he say anything before shooting himself?"

"Honestly Toya, I don't know whether to feel sorry for the man or continue to be angry with him for pulling us into his drama." Shaking his head, Jarrod continued. "He tagged you and me to his live video. He said that we left him no choice. That he was right in front of the police station to turn himself in. All he asked was that we help his wife... do what we promised. Then he shot himself."

"Oh, my God." Toya clamped her hand over her mouth and just shook her head. "What was he thinking?"

Standing back up, Jarrod told her, "I have no idea. But I plan to find out. I'm going to see if dad will ride out to the hospital with me. I'll call you later to let you know what's going on."

A buzzer rang, Jarrod looked around as Toya got up and pressed a button on the wall next to her garage. "Hello."

"Your groceries are here."

"Let them in, Larry. Thank you."

"Right away, Ms. Toya."

"I thought grocery delivery was for old ladies and people who broke a limb or something." Jarrod gave her a puzzled look.

"It's just convenient for me. I'm not working right now, so why should I go out for groceries when they have a service to bring it to me?" The doorbell rang.

Toya made a big production about asking for identification and for the person to give her the total amount of her order before she opened the door and took the groceries from them.

Jarrod stood up and took the bags from the delivery driver. As Toya closed the door, he put her bags on the kitchen counter. "I'm going to get going. I'll call you later and let you know what I find out."

"Thanks for doing this Jarrod. I really don't think I could deal with seeing Deacon Brown like that right now."

"Yeah, I'm beginning to understand that." He kissed her on the forehead and left.

~~~

By the time they arrived at the hospital, Deacon Brown was just waking from surgery. Thomas pressed the intercom button to be buzzed into the ICU.

"May I help you?" the voice on the other side of the intercom asked.

"I'm here to see Clarence Brown."

"Are you immediate family?"

"I'm his pastor," Thomas replied. They hadn't seen so much as the back of Brown's head in the last six months. But his name was still on the roll books, so technically, Thomas and Yvonne Reed were still his pastors.

She gave them the room number, then unlocked the door. Thomas and Jarrod began walking down the corridor in search of room number eleven. "We will pray for him, get his wife's information, and then get out of here."

Jarrod agreed. "I know I should have more compassion for a man who just tried to kill himself. But I'm still so angry about him tagging Toya to that video that I just want to shake him."

"I feel the same way, son. I'm boiling inside about you seeing such a thing. But I'm also thankful you were able to spare Toya. She's gone through enough." Thomas shook his head at the whole maddening mess. "But God says different, and I've got to go with what my spirit man wants rather than what my flesh wants to do right now."

Jarrod took a deep breath and patted his father on the shoulder as they arrived in front of Deacon Brown's room. Jarrod walked behind his father as they entered the room. Deacon Brown's eyes had been closed, but like a man on the run, those eyes popped open the moment he heard the squeak of the door.

"I knew you'd come," he said, then his eyes fell to the pressure of the meds and drooped. He went back to sleep.

Jarrod and Thomas sat down. After a minute, Jarrod whispered, "Should we wake him?"

Thomas shook his head. "He looked like he's been through the wringer these last few months. He probably needs to rest."

"He does look a lot older. I was a little shocked when we walked through the door."

"I'm a cautionary tale in the flesh, young man," Deacon Brown's voice was groggy as he tried to open his eyes again. "You don't ever want to be like me."

"You seemed like a good man when I hung out with you as a teenager. I just don't know what happened to you?" As soon as Jarrod said those words, he remembered that his father didn't want to get into all that with Deacon Brown. He lifted a hand, like waving the white flag. "But we're not here to talk about that."

Thomas stood and walked over to the bed. "We wanted to pray with you and then see how we can help Mildred."

Brown's face contorted as if he was in pain and a tear rolled down the side of his face. "After all I've done to your family. I don't have a right to receive prayer from you, pastor. It's over for me. Just help my Mildred."

"None of us have a right to expect anything from God. We have all sinned and done so much wrong in the sight of a Holy God. But He still wants to forgive us, heal us, and make us whole. If you can believe with me for a moment." Thomas took Brown's hand. "Then we can go before God and ask him to help you and Mildred."

"Okay Pastor, let's do that."

Jarrod stood on the opposite side of the bed from his father. He put Brown's free hand in his then offered his right hand to his father. As his dad took his hand, Jarrod noticed that the patch on Brown's head did not extend to the back of his head but just went from the front to the left, just above the ear.

Jarrod had assumed that the bullet would have come out the back of his head, but it must have just grazed the front, and exited out of

22

the side of his head by the left ear. That's probably what saved Brown's life.

Thomas prayed, "Lord God, we humbly come to You now, realizing that our fate is in Your hands and that You know the number of our days. How great You are... how wise You are. Lord, we trust You, and we ask that You do something miraculous in Clarence and Mildred's lives. Change them from the inside out. We ask that You heal our sister Mildred...

Jarrod's eyes were closed as he listened to his father bring heaven right in the room with them. That was how he felt each and every time Thomas Reed opened his mouth to pray. Jarrod wondered why it never felt as if the earth was about to shake when he prayed. He sometimes questioned if God really heard his prayers because he didn't get that special feeling he always had when his dad prayed.

"Thank You, Father, for Your goodness, thank You for Your grace," Thomas continued. "We will always give You praise. We stand in awe of Your greatness. Do those great and marvelous things that You do. Again, we thank You, in Jesus name we pray, and we count it done. Amen."

That was the other thing about his father's prayers. He always ended them with such authority... Jarrod would never be so presumptuous to 'count it done.' To Jarrod, that was like telling God He had better do it or else. Jarrod thought it was better to ask, and just hope that God felt like helping him out. But maybe that was the reason he didn't feel the earth move when he prayed. Maybe his father just believed more than he did.

3

"Dad, let me ask you something," Jarrod said as he drove Thomas back to his house.

"Ask away, my number one son."

Jarrod smiled at the term 'number one son.' When in fact he was Thomas Reed's only son. That fact didn't change even after marrying Yvonne, because Yvonne only had two daughters. And one of them was in some kind of trouble. "Have you noticed anything different about Toya?"

"Toya?" Thomas' eyebrows scrunched. "Can't say that I've noticed anything, but she hasn't been around that much lately."

"That's because she doesn't leave her house that much. She quit her job at the law firm, sits at home in her PJs all day, and she is even having her groceries delivered."

"That's not like Toya. She's always been so outgoing and ready to take on the world. This thing with Marvel must be affecting her even more than we thought." Thomas shook his head. "We've all been so busy these last few months with mine and Yvonne's wedding, then Tia and Robbie, I don't think any of us noticed that Toya was having problems."

"Didn't you think something was wrong when she moved into this high-security place and then quit her job?"

Thomas shook his head. "I'm the one who told her about that condo. I think it's the best place for a young, single woman."

They came to a red light. Jarrod pulled up to the light and stopped the car then glanced over at his father. "Okay, Dad, the condo makes sense. But having her groceries delivered and quitting her job, without having another job lined up?"

"I'm glad you brought this to my attention, son. Yvonne and I will pray and figure out the best way to help Toya through this situation. But you've got to understand her fear because it's been six months since Marvel attacked her and the police still haven't found him."

Jarrod rounded the corner and pulled into his father's driveway. He put the car in park and then turned to his father. "One last question, Dad."

"Shoot."

"Why do your prayers seemed to shake the earth, but when I pray, it's like nothing is happening. I don't feel anything at all. Don't even know if God is listening to me."

Thomas smiled; his eyes drifted a bit as if he was thinking of a long-ago memory. "I used to think the same thing about my father's prayers. You know what he told me about it."

"Gramps used to talk my ear off, so I can only imagine what he had to say."

"Most preachers are big talkers. But his answer was really short and sweet. When I asked how come his prayers seemed to touch heaven when mine sputtered out before I got off my knees, he just looked at me and said, 'keep living.'"

Jarrod didn't understand. "You for real, that's all he said?"

"Son, it was more than a mouthful. Because I came to understand that in my early years, I hadn't experienced all the things in life that could break your heart and knock you down. I didn't know what it was like to pray to God whenever things were on the line, and if God didn't come through, I would be lost... but I kept on living, and I found out.

"Now, do I wish pain and heartache on you?" Thomas shook his head as he opened the door and got out of the car. He then lowered his head so that he was looking directly at Jarrod. "Life won't always be easy for you. And I can't promise to be here when you run into trouble. But if you find that secret place in God, I can promise that your prayers will shake the foundation of heaven and God's angels will move on your behave."

~~~

Jarrod figured that while his dad was praying for Toya, he would do something that would motivate her to get out of the house. There was no surprising her since he had to be buzzed in at the gate, but at least she would be surprised by what he had in his possession.

"Come on, girl. I want to introduce you to the most beautiful woman I know. And that's inside and out. You'll see." Jarrod kept talking to the dog as if he understood and was going to give feedback.

He rang the doorbell and tried to wait quietly at Toya's front door, but one of Toya's neighbors was jogging down the street with her dog, and his three-month-old puppy started barking her head off and trying desperately to get off her leash. Jarrod scooped her into his arms. "Calm down, they aren't the enemy."

"What is all this noise out here?" Toya asked as she swung the door wide open.

"Sorry about that. She's a protector by nature."

26

Toya reached out and rubbed the dog's ears. "Where'd you get a dog from?"

They walked inside the apartment. Toya closed the door and locked the deadbolt. Jarrod sat the puppy down. "I got her at a shelter. Unfortunately, her owner passed away a couple of weeks ago. I felt so bad that I had to take her. But now I don't know what I'm going to do with her."

The dog slow walked over to Toya. Sniffed her leg, then circled around her. "What's the dilemma?"

"My rental doesn't allow pets. My lease is up in two months. I can move to another spot after that. But until then, I need to find someone to keep her."

Toya and Jarrod took a seat in the living room. The dog sat down at Toya's feet, and without noticing what she was doing, Toya started rubbing the dog's fur. "What's her name?"

"Princess... I've got all her paperwork. She's been well taken care of."

"Now, why do I feel like I'm being set up for something?"

With a crooked smile, Jarrod said, "I'm not trying to set you up. But Princess does seem to like you... and you like her." He pointed toward Toya's left hand. "You haven't stopped rubbing her since we sat down. And you are the only full-grown person I know who doesn't have a job."

"Ooooh, low blow." Toya took one of the pillows off her sofa and tossed it at Jarrod's head. "And how do you expect me to get a job if I'm stuck watching your dog?"

"She's a German Shepherd, Toya. These kind of dogs are very trainable. She won't take a dump in the house if you show her what to do."

"I'm not buying your sales pitch." But Princess cocked her head to the side as she stared at Toya. Looking into the dog's eyes, Toya thought she saw them water. "Don't you start too."

Princess whimpered and then laid her head on Toya's lap.

"How can you say no to her. She practically loves you already."

"Well…" Toya rubbed the dogs head. "I guess I can dog sit for you. But you need to purchase all her food and supplies… I don't have a job, remember?"

"I'm already on it." Jarrod went back to his car and popped the trunk. He grabbed hold of a huge bag, swung it on his back and carried it into Toya's townhouse like he was Santa Claus bringing gifts.

Laughing as Jarrod dumped his bag of goodies on her living room floor, Toya asked, "What did you do? Buy everything in the doggie section of the store?"

"Well, she's a puppy, so she's going to need her doggie bed, right?" Jarrod pulled the doggie bed out of the bag. He then pulled a bone out of the bag and threw it towards Princess. "That's so she doesn't chew up your furniture. I got her a couple more chew toys too."

"Let me look in this bag." Toya started going through the items in the bag. "She's got enough dog food to last a month. Oh, and I like this dual food and water container. Perfect." Toya sat the food and water bowl set on the floor, she then tried to pull the humongous bag of food out of the bag, but it was too heavy. "You need to take that bag of doggie food to the kitchen. I'm going to have to find a big spoon to dip the food out with because I certainly can't lift that bag every day."

They took all the items out of the bag together. Jarrod carried the dog food bag to the kitchen, and Toya carried the doggie bed to her bedroom. Princess was just a pup, so she didn't want her sleeping alone in a new environment.

The doggie toys were scattered throughout the house because Toya wanted to introduce Princess to her toys in each room, so the dog would know what she could chew on and what she couldn't, like her brand-new sofa. Chewing on that sofa would get Princess put out.

When she and Jarrod sat back down, Toya told him. "I expect you to share parenting duties with me. So, you need to come by and help me train this dog. I don't want her peeing and dumping all over the floor."

Jarrod smiled. "I was going to offer to do that anyway because there are a few things I want to teach her."

"Good then, we're on the same page."

Still smiling, Jarrod said, "Not quite, but close enough."

4

"Penny for your thoughts," Thomas said as he walked into the bedroom.

Yvonne was perched on the edge of the bed staring at the wall in front of her. She had a sorrowful look on her face when she turned to her husband. "I was just wondering how I could have missed it… I mean, I know my daughters… Tia is the one who always seems to need help getting out of her own way. But Toya has always been the strong one. I even leaned on her shoulders many nights after their dad died."

Thomas sat down next to his wife. They weren't new to this husband and wife thing. They both had been married to wonderful people with marriages that lasted over twenty-five years. But now that their first loves had passed away, Thomas and Yvonne were discovering that second chance love was just as good as the first go around.

He took Yvonne's hand in his. "You can't do this to yourself, baby. Toya has been hiding this from us. I'm just thankful that Jarrod was so observant."

Yvonne shook her head. "This takes me right back to Tia and Toya's high school days. I was so busy flying all over the world trying to become this renowned, sought after preacher, so I could prove to David that I truly belonged behind the pulpit that I missed so many special moments.

"I'm convinced that Tia gave up on college because she figured I wouldn't notice any of her accomplishments anyway."

"No," Thomas interrupted her pity party. "Tia decided on art school because she is an artist. That's the gift God gave her. And you are a preacher, so you were doing what God called you to do as well."

A tear of regret drifted down Yvonne's beautiful face. "I tried really hard not to miss too many special moments, but I should have been there more. And I should have recognized that Toya is struggling because of what that evil man did to her."

"I'm not going to let you do this to yourself. We've been praying, and God is going to bring her through this. Now do you trust the God you've been serving all these years and even gave up special moments with your kids to do His will, or not?" Thomas was firm with her, because he didn't want her to fall apart, not when they had such a hefty task at hand.

"I believe, Thomas. I really do. But I just can't stand knowing that my child is dealing with fear so bad that she wants to shut herself off from the world." Yvonne rubbed the front of her forehead as if she were trying to massage something that made sense into her head. "Has this man also destroyed her trust in God's ability to protect her?"

"I'll tell you how we can find out... let's go ask her?"

Yvonne smiled at her husband. "I knew you would say that, and I love you for it. But I heard God clearly say 'wait.' Believe me, I want to rush over there and tell her to pack her bags and come home with us. But if what I want to do will get in God's way, then I can't do it."

"Then we'll wait," Thomas agreed and then got on his knees and prayed.

"Love you for this too," Yvonne whispered as she got on her knees and joined her husband in prayer.

~~~

Marvel Williams hung up the phone with a sinister smirk on his face. Toya had quit her job and moved out of the condo she owned when they were dating. She thought she could make herself invisible so that he couldn't find her. But her days of hiding were numbered, just as his days of hiding would soon come to an end. Yvonne Milner-Reed would one day know how it truly feels to lose someone you love.

He had come so close to giving Yvonne just what she had coming to her. He leaned back in his chair and allowed himself to relive the day he almost got even with her…

Marvel sat outside of Toya's office and smiled as he watched his lovely girlfriend—soon-to-be ex-girlfriend—rush out of her office building. He removed his pistol from the glove compartment, stuffed it in his waistband, and stepped out of the car.

Toya slowed her pace when she noticed him standing by the trunk of his car. She frowned but then recovered and gave him a warm smile.

"What are you doing here? And why didn't you tell me you were waiting for me?" She turned her head to the left, then right, as if she were looking for someone.

His smile matched hers. "I wanted to surprise you, baby. We haven't spent much time together, and I was missing my boo."

She gave him a hug and kissed him on the cheek. "So, do you want to leave your car here and ride with me to the restaurant?"

"No, I want you to get in my car," he said, still smiling.

"I don't want to leave my car at the office. Why don't you just follow me?" She looked around the parking lot again.

Marvel wrapped his hand around Toya's arm, gently at first, but as he opened his jacket and showed her his gun, he tightened his grip. "Get in my car now, Toya."

"W-what's the problem, Marvel?"

"Get in the car." He shoved her toward the passenger door.

"All right, all right. You don't have to push."

"And you didn't have to betray me," he said as he opened the door, shoved her inside, and slammed it shut.

He locked the car from the outside, then ran around to the driver's door and unlocked it so that he could get in. Turning the key in the ignition, he said, "I hate to spoil your dinner, but I have other plans for you."

"What's wrong with you, Marvel? Will you at least tell me what's going on?" Her eyes were wild with fear.

"Why didn't you tell me that you read that e-mail from Clarence Brown? If we're in a relationship, then we shouldn't keep secrets, Toya."

"What are you talking about?" she screamed. "Have you lost your mind or something? You'll go to jail for kidnapping me!"

"Who am I kidnapping? You just called and invited me to dinner. Remember?"

"I didn't ask to be shoved into your car at gunpoint."

"Hey, this is just the way we get down. You know how we do it, how we joke around and kid with each other. And as soon as I get you to my house, I'm going to kid around with you a little more...

after I tie you up." He smiled at her as if he were offering to draw her a bubble bath.

"Why are you doing this, Marvel? I thought we really had something."

"I'm just getting you before you get me. Do you think I really believed that you wanted to have dinner with me?" He looked at her. *"What were you going to do, put something in my drink to knock me out so that I wouldn't be able to make it to the City Council meeting?"*

Toya didn't respond.

"You and your mother thought you were going to rat me out at this meeting tonight, but I'm about to change the good pastor's mind."

"And how are you going to do that?" Toya defiantly asked, as if she weren't riding with a man with a gun in his pants.

"Call her."

"No."

Marvel pulled the gun out of his waistband and pointed it at Toya. *"Call your mother."*

"What did she ever do to you? Why are you trying to destroy her ministry?"

"It's personal. Now call," he barked.

Toya pulled her cell phone out of her purse, pressed a button, and held the phone with a shaking hand to her ear. Several seconds later, she said, *"Mama, I'm so sorry. I should have listened to you."*

"Hand me that phone," Marvel said. He snatched it away from Toya, who had started crying in a high-pitched, panicked sort of way. *"Hey, Pastor Yvonne,"* he said coolly. *"This is Marvel."*

"What do you want?" Yvonne shrieked. *"What are you doing with my daughter?"*

"She's my girlfriend, remember?"

When Yvonne didn't reply to that, Marvel continued. "Anyway, I just wanted you to know that Toya is going to be otherwise occupied until after the City Council meeting. I'm the only one who knows where she'll be, so I suggest that you think long and hard before sharing anything about my business dealings at this meeting tonight."

"He's got a gun," Toya screamed.

"Don't you hurt my daughter!" Yvonne yelled.

He held his hand to the back of Toya's head and gently moved it down her neck. "Oh, I could never hurt Toya. But you can...just as you always hurt innocent people. It's up to you, Pastor Yvonne." He hoped that she could hear the depth of his contempt. "Is Toya going to get hurt? You decide."

"You do realize that you are going to be arrested, right?" Toya assured him when he hung up the phone. "There is no way out of this but prison."

Driving down the street like a dope man running from the law, Marvel said, "If I'm in prison, but you're dead, which one of us is better off?"

"Why are you doing this, Marvel? What did I ever do to you?" Toya was screaming at him. Anger flashed in her eyes.

But Marvel had just as much anger and attitude. "You betrayed me, that's what you did. Just like my mother betrayed my father. And I'm going to give you just what he gave her."

"I don't have anything to do with what happened between your mother and father."

"Oh, yes, you do. Your mother is the reason my mother is dead, and my father is still in prison."

"That's ridiculous, Marvel. My mother doesn't even know your parents!" Toya screamed.

Marvel drove wildly through the streets of Detroit. He'd made so many swerves and U-turns that he'd almost forgotten where he was trying to go. "Your mother wrote that stupid book, *Girl, Free Yourself!*" he screamed back at her as he made another U-turn. "And my mother read it!"

Toya rolled her eyes. "So what? I don't see the relevance."

"You wouldn't," Marvel sneered. "But my weak-minded mother suddenly found the strength to leave my father after reading that idiotic book by Pastor Yvonne." He spoke Yvonne's name as if it were poison that he needed to spit out of his mouth before it killed him.

"My mother didn't have anything to do with what your mother did."

"She didn't put the gun in my father's hand, either, but he still killed my mother. And I still blame yours."

"That's totally irrational," Toya said.

"It might be irrational to you, but it's all that I've thought about since the day my father was sentenced to prison." He pulled up in front of an abandoned house on Rosa Parks Boulevard and gave Toya a lopsided grin. "Honey, we're home."

"Home? What are you talking about?" Toya frantically looked around.

"Come on, baby, this is where the magic happens." He opened the driver's door, grabbed hold of her arm, and pulled her out of the car with him.

"You don't want to do this, Marvel." She tried to pull away, but he was too strong. "You are a brilliant man. Why do you want to ruin your life like this?"

"Shut up!" He hit her with the butt of the gun, then drug her into the house and tied her up.

Victory had been in sight. Marvel knew that once he had killed Toya and Yvonne was in misery, he would finally be rid of this all-consuming hatred and anger that guided his every move. But something crazy that Marvel still didn't understand caused all of his plans to come crashing down on him.

He hadn't been able to destroy Yvonne, and now he was a wanted man. All of his legal assets had been frozen. He was thankful that the authorities didn't know about the money he kept in the Cayman Islands. It was just enough to keep him afloat until he could get back to Detroit and finish what he started... and nothing would stop him this time. And if there were a God in heaven who was looking after the Milners, He too would lose this next fight.

5

"How is Jayden. I miss that baby so much," Toya said after answering her sister, Tia's phone call.

"I'm glad you miss her, big sis. Because I need your help."

"Ask away." Toya got up from her desk, looked around her home office for her house shoes. She hated walking on hardwood floors barefoot. But as usual, Princess was laying on top of her house shoes. "Get up, Princess. I need those shoes."

The dog just stared at her but didn't move. "Whatever." Toya threw up her hands in frustration and then headed to the kitchen barefooted.

"Who are you talking to?"

"My dog."

"When did you get a dog?"

"I didn't. Actually, Princess belongs to Jarrod. But it's a long story, girl. Just tell me what you need."

"Robbie has a job interview in Nashville, so he's going to be gone all night. I was hoping that you could spend the night with us."

"Why is Robbie on a job interview? Don't tell me he got fired again?"

"No, nothing like that. He's actually interviewing for a management position. It would be a promotion. But he has to go to Nashville because the company's headquarters is there."

"That's awesome, Tia." Toya didn't want to leave her environment, where she felt safe and secure. But she couldn't ask Tia to pack all the stuff she would need for herself and a five-month-old baby. "Okay, let me get Jarrod to do some dog sitting for his own dog, and I'll see you two later this evening."

Jarrod was at work, so she left him a message and then finished making her sandwich. Just as she was about to sit down and eat it, Princess went into the mudroom, pulled down her leash, and sat it in front of Toya.

"Ah, come on," Toya rolled her eyes heavenward. "How are you smart enough to grab a leash when you want to go outside, but you can't stop laying on my house shoes. And why do you even need to go out again? I just took you out three hours ago."

Princess lifted her paws as she sat up and whimpered.

"You're worse than having a kid. My goodness, how can I even think about getting a job when I have to walk you four times a day." Toya put the leash on Princess and then took her outside.

The daily walk, times four were actually very relaxing for Toya. The first couple of times she had to take Princess out, she was so worried about walking around the corner that she almost called Jarrod and told him to take Princess somewhere else. But when she looked into those watery eyes, she just couldn't give her back. So, she took her outside. Toya was careful to check her surroundings at first. But now that she and Princess had been on their routine for almost two weeks, she forgot all about checking her surroundings and began to enjoy the walks.

"You had to pee really bad, didn't you, girl?" Before Tia called, Toya had been in her kitchen, making a sandwich and daydreaming about how life used to be when she actually had a life. She had once been a lawyer climbing her way up the corporate ladder, now she was just a dog sitter. While she had been feeling sorry for herself, Princess kept trying to get her attention, but Toya was too busy trying to come up with her next move that she hadn't noticed Princess until the dog got right in her face and begged to go out. "I'm sorry I ignored you. It won't happen again."

Just as Princess was finishing and they were about to walk further down the block, someone tapped Toya on the shoulder. At that moment, Toya almost peed her pants in the very spot Princess had just used. How could she have let her guard down like this? Why hadn't she checked her surrounding before letting Princess do her business?

"Toya! I can't believe it's you," the voice exclaimed with joy.

Instantly, there was a feeling of familiarity. She knew that voice. Toya turned around and found herself face-to-face with her best friend from high school. She hadn't seen Gina Melson since graduation. They swore they would keep in touch, but they enrolled in different colleges that were in different states. Then, they never seemed to be home from college at the same time.

Then when Toya discovered that Gina had started dating Jarrod, that ended it for Toya. Her two best friends were attending the same college and falling in love, and even though Toya had been hundreds of miles away, she felt like a third wheel, so she distanced herself from both of them.

Jarrod was now back in her life thanks to Thomas marrying her mother, and she had just run into Gina. "You here visiting your parents?" Toya asked, holding Princess's leash tightly.

Gina shook her head. "Not this time. I moved back here a month ago."

"That's good to know," Toya said and meant it. For years she had missed having both Jarrod and Gina in her life. "Are you staying with your parents?"

Gina pointed toward the townhouse in front of them. "Moved in last week."

"Wow! I live in this community too. My building is right around the corner."

Princess barked and started yanking her leash forward.

"You must work from home to be able to walk your dog in the middle of the afternoon."

"Something like that." Princess yanked the leash again. "Let me finish walking this dog." Toya gave Gina her address. "If you have time, stop by, I should be back in a few minutes."

"I just might do that." Gina opened her car door and took two bags of groceries out. "Let me unload this, and I'll come hang out with you for a minute."

True to her word, Gina was at Toya's door within twenty minutes. Toya grabbed a bag of Lays chips from the pantry. She took the onion dip out of the fridge. "Do you still like orange sodas?" She asked while the fridge was still open.

"I'm strictly on water these days. I did a sugar fast a few years ago and haven't gone back since."

"So, you've gotten healthy on me." Toya held up the chip bag. "Do I need to put this back and get the celery instead."

"Oh no, I haven't gotten over my love of Lays chips, which is one of the reasons I run a couple of miles every day."

"Such discipline. I wish I had it. Whenever I'm feeling down, I eat a half bag of these chips with this onion dip."

"Well, it isn't affecting you at all. Looks like you weigh the same as you did when we were in high school."

Toya laughed. "I passed that fifteen pounds ago." She put the chips in a bowl, handed Gina a bottle of water and then sat the chips and dip in front of them as they took a seat in the living room.

Gina scooped a few chips in her hand and dipped one. "You're hiding those extra pounds well because I can't tell you've gained anything at all. Now me, on the other hand, I'm shaped like an apple, so when I start gaining weight, it shows up in my belly first. Which is not good, so I work hard to keep those dreaded pounds away."

Toya sat down on the sofa with Gina. Before they knew it, two hours had gone by, the bowl had three chips left. "You want another bottle of water?" Toya asked as she got up to add more soda and ice to her glass.

"No, I'm good." Gina held up her bottle to show that she still had some water. "But you know what I'm curious about?"

"What?"

"Okay, I get that you're not married, just like me but I don't understand why?"

Toya wasn't ready to discuss Marvel with Gina just yet. In their two-hour conversation, they had talked about many things, but not the most horrific parts of her life. So, she simply shrugged and said, "Just haven't met the right man, I guess."

"But you've known him all your life, Toya. I just don't get why things didn't work out with you and Jarrod."

"Me and Jarrod?" Toya looked at Gina as if she had suddenly grown two heads. "You and Jarrod were a couple in college, remember?"

Gina drank the rest of her water and then joined Toya in the kitchen. "Oh, I remember alright. All he did was talk about you every time we were together. We barely even kissed, because Jarrod didn't really want me as his girlfriend. He wanted someone he could share memories of you with."

"That's crazy, Gina. You and Jarrod both told me that you were dating."

"I think Jarrod thought he wanted to date me at first, but when you stopped calling us and wouldn't accept our phone calls, things really got bad for him. He mopped around campus and even threatened to call your mom to talk some sense into you."

A look of embarrassment crossed Toya's face as she handed Gina another bottle of water. "So, y'all knew that I was mad?"

Gina nodded. "I tried calling you so many times. I thought for sure that when you came home for Christmas our junior year that you would call me, and things would go back to the way they had been. But I never heard from you."

Toya tapped on her forehead as she went back in time, trying to remember what she was doing. "Wait a minute. I did come home that Christmas. And I saw Jarrod and his family, but he didn't tell me that you two weren't dating anymore. Nor did he attempt to ask me out."

"I can't believe that. Before we left school for our break, I made him promise that he would fess up about how he felt about you. I can't believe he chickened out like that." Shaking her head, Gina then said, "Now everything makes sense."

"You're losing me again." Toya had been completely caught off guard by the whole conversation. Jarrod had never expressed any interest in her. He treated her like a little sister.

"All I know is Jarrod changed when he came back to school. He rarely spoke to me, then he started dating all these random women like he needed to prove something to himself. I honestly thought he would get it together once you and he started dating."

"We've never dated," Toya practically screamed the words.

"Wow." Gina's eyes widened as she tried to make sense of what she had heard. Then she asked, "Did he ever slow down and get married?"

Toya shook her head. "Still dating a bunch of big boob women."

Gina laughed at that. "I don't remember if the women he dated in college were big breasted, I just know that there were so many that I eventually stopped counting and started minding my own business."

"Same here." Toya pointed toward Princess. "I even let him turn me into a dog sitter so he could have all his free time for the ladies."

"Well, at least you two are friends again."

"That doesn't bother you, does it?"

"Of course not. I told you, Jarrod and I were never a thing. Believe me, Jarrod was not the love of my life. Sometimes I wish he had been. He has a good heart."

The way Gina said that made Toya think that whoever her friend had fallen in love with, the man must have been some kind of monster. Right then she wanted to spill the beans about the monster in her own life.

Gina looked at the time on her cell phone. "It is getting late. I've got to get going."

"Don't be a stranger," Toya said as she walked her to the door.

"Same to you. I showed you where my house is, so the next visit is on you." Just as she was walking out the door, Gina turned back to Toya and said, "I really needed this. So glad I ran into you today. Please don't ignore my calls this time."

They had exchanged phone numbers during their conversation. Both of them had locked each other's contact info in their phones. "I won't, I promise."

6

"You had company today?" Jarrod asked when he noticed two paper plates on the living room table and a big bowl with a few chips in it.

Toya's head swiveled around like she had been caught. "Huh, what?"

He pointed at the coffee table while he put the leash on Princess. "You've got two plates over there."

"Oh yeah, right." She snapped her finger as if she'd almost forgotten her entire afternoon. "Thanks to Princess, I ran into someone while I was on one of my four walks per day with her."

"How did Princess act while you were talking to your neighbor?"

Toya shrugged. "Princess was peeing when I was tapped on the shoulder. I have to admit, I almost peed right there too. My heart was beating so fast, that if it had been a man standing there when I turned around, I probably would have passed out."

"But Princess barked at her, right?"

Toya shook her head. "She kinda whimpered when I stood there talking too long. She wanted to find her spot to take her dump."

"So, you're telling me that somebody approached you on the street, tapped on your shoulder and Princess didn't even bark at them?" Jarrod couldn't believe what he was hearing. He bought this dog because they were known protectors.

"She wasn't exactly random. I've known her for a long time, just haven't seen her in a while."

"Wow!" Jarrod got down on a knee in front Princess and spoke to the dog like she was human. "We've got a lot of work to do, don't we girl?" He turned back to Toya. "I need a t-shirt or sweater that you have worn recently."

"Trust me, with those biceps, none of my shirts will fit you."

"Hahaha," he gave her a fake laugh, then with a serious look on his face, he said, "I need the shirt."

"Okay, geesh. You don't have to be so touchy I was just joking." Toya went into her bedroom and took the t-shirt she wore earlier in the day out of the laundry and handed it to Jarrod.

"Thanks." He took the shirt and put it under the dog's nose. "You smell that? That's Toya?"

"I don't have a smell," Toya said, offended at the notion that she smelled.

"Everyone has a scent. Yours just happens to be a light florally scent."

"I smell like flowers, huh?"

"You do to me." He looked up at her. Their eyes locked. Jarrod felt heat like a fire had started at his feet and drifted all the way up to his heart. He was a fool for loving a woman who wanted nothing to do with him. Jarrod turned back to the dog.

Princess was standing on all fours, Jarrod said, "Sit." Then helped the dog put her back two legs into a sitting position. "Get me her treats."

Toya went into the kitchen and took a bag of doggie treats out of the cabinet and brought them back to Jarrod.

Princess was once again standing on all fours. Jarrod said, "Sit." And the dog sat.

"Oh, my goodness. She did it." Toya was excited to see that Princess actually listened to commands.

Jarrod handed her a treat. "Good doggie," he said as he rubbed the dogs head. He then stood up and stepped away from the dog. Jarrod pointed to the spot in front of him and said, "Come here."

Princess trotted over to the spot, Jarrod pointed at. Jarrod then said, "Sit." And she did. "Good doggie." He rubbed her head again and handed her another treat.

"She actually listens. I can't believe it. Do you know how many times I've tried to get her to get off of my house shoes? She lays on them and won't give them back."

"I think she's just messing with you. Come over here." Jarrod reached for Toya, she put her hand in his and then stood in front of Princess with him. Jarrod held onto her hand just a moment longer than necessary.

Toya dropped his hand. "Okay, so what do you want me to do?"

"Tell her to bark."

Toya gave Jarrod a questioning glance. "She's not going to bark just because I tell her to."

"Just try it."

"Bark," Toya said in a lackluster manner."

Princess just stared at her.

"Do it again and be serious with it this time." He handed her a treat. "Let her see it."

"Okayyyy." Toya playfully shoved Jarrod. Then held up the treat in front of Princess and said, more authoritatively this time, "Bark."

Princess barked.

"Hand her the treat." Toya tossed the treat in Princess's mouth. Jarrod rubbed the dog's back. "Good girl."

Toya snapped her finger. "I should have said, good girl to her when I gave her the treat, right?"

"Yes, you want to reward her with a treat and affirm her with your words and actions when she does something you want her to do. German Shepherds are smart dogs, and they catch on quickly as long as you're not sending them mix messages."

"Yeah, mix messages are a terrible thing," Toya said as she walked away from Jarrod. She went into her bedroom and rolled her suitcase out. "Well, you have fun with Princess tonight."

"I will. And thanks for letting me stay here tonight. My complex is such a stickler on this no pet issue. I just don't want to lose my deposit when I move out of there next month."

"Clean up behind yourself, and I'll see both of you tomorrow."

"Give Tia and Jayden a hug and kiss from me."

~~~

Holding Jayden in her arms, Toya felt more at peace than she had in the last six months. She was apprehensive about leaving her community where she felt safe, but now she was so glad that she had come. "Look how big she has gotten. My goodness, it seems like it was just yesterday that I was rocking her to sleep, and she felt so tiny in my arms. Now she's like a butterball."

"That's because it wasn't yesterday. You haven't seen Jayden in three months."

That couldn't be true. Had she actually let three months go by without seeing her precious niece? What would happen if Robbie got the promotion and they moved all the way to Nashville? She had to do better as a sister and an aunt. "I'm sorry sis, I hadn't realized that I had let so much time go by."

"You just better be glad that Jayden still remembers you," Tia scolded.

"You could visit me too, you know?"

Tia shook her head. "We're down to one car right now, and with Robbie's schedule, it's hard for me to get the car for anything but grocery store runs and doctor's appointments."

"Sounds like y'all are making it work though."

"Robbie's frustrated that he doesn't earn enough to get me a car, but I told him that while I'm at home with Jayden, I don't have that many places to go anyway."

"How soon would you have to move to Nashville if he gets the job?" Toya hated even the thought of her baby sister and niece moving to Tennessee, but if they are struggling financially and this promotion would help their money situation, then how could she stand in the way.

"The management position is at his plant. We won't have to move if he gets the job. But he might have to attend quarterly meetings at headquarters."

"That's even better." Now, Toya was truly excited for them. She prayed that Robbie received this promotion so he could do everything that was in his heart for his family.

Tia made green tea for her and Toya and sat a plate of the Toll House cookies that she had baked on the table in front of them.

"Are those pecan turtle delights?"

"Girl, you know I got you. When you told me you were spending the night, I picked a pack up after I dropped Robbie off at the airport."

Happily munching on a cookie, Toya told her sister, "I haven't had one of these in months. I keep forgetting to order these cookies."

"Why don't you just pick it up at the store when you do your grocery shopping?"

Toya hesitated for a moment, picking up her tea, she took a sip. Growing up as a church girl, Toya hated lying, so she took a deep breath and admitted, "To tell you the truth, I've been having my groceries delivered."

"Are you kidding?" Tia's eyes lit up.

Toya braced herself for the judgment to come. No one understood why she needed to have her groceries delivered. It wasn't like she had a broken leg or was a senior citizen as Jarrod informed her.

"My grocery store down the street just started doing delivery. I would love to do that, but I just don't like the idea of paying the delivery fee, especially when it cost more than the gas I would use to drive over there."

Toya didn't want to get into it, so she changed the subject. "Guess who I ran into today, you'll never guess."

"Well then, go ahead and tell me."

"Gina."

Tia looked puzzled, then her eyes brightened as she asked, "Your best friend from high school? That, Gina?"

"You have a good memory. And yes, that Gina. She moved back to town and now lives in the same community as I do."

Jayden had fallen to sleep, Tia took her to the bedroom and laid her in her crib. When she came back to the family room with Toya, she said, "So what has Gina been up to?"

"It sounds like she is doing well in her career. She's a marketing consulting and has just opened her own firm."

"That's awesome. I always wondered about her and about what happened to the two of you. I mean, y'all had been so close."

"Yeah, it was my fault. I was a stupid kid back then. But I am glad that I ran into her. Hopefully, we can become friends again." Toya wanted to tell Tia what Gina had said about Jarrod coming home for Christmas during their junior year of college to confess his love for her. But since it never happened, Toya felt silly mentioning it. Still, she wondered why Jarrod told Gina that if he didn't plan on doing it?

7

When Toya arrived home the next day, Jarrod was still training Princess. At first, she thought everything he was doing was cute. He was just a dog owner trying to show off his pup. But then he told her that one of his friends was on their way over and he needed her to allow him through the gate.

"So, now you're having company at my place?"

"Nothing like that. I need to train Princess on something, and I need a stranger for this."

When the man arrived. Toya buzzed him through the gate. She expected Jarrod to open the door and let the man in, but instead when the man stepped to the door, Jarrod turned to Princess.

"You hear that girl?"

The man peeked in the picture window next to the door, Princess's head shot up. She immediately started barking, and the man ran off. In the next minute the man was back at the door, but this time he didn't peek through the window, he twisted the doorknob.

Princess's head shot up again, she barked and rushed toward the door.

"Enough, Princess," Jarrod said, and the dog stopped barking. "Good doggie." Out came the treats as Jarrod sat down next to the dog, handed her the treat, and then rubbed her like she had done something extra special. Then Jarrod said, "It's you and Toya against everybody outside of this place. You protect her, okay girl."

As Toya watched Jarrod and Princess, she became acutely aware of something. Her hands went to her hips. "Hey, this isn't your dog at all, is she?"

"What?" Jarrod turned to face Toya. "So, now you think I'm a dog thief?"

"Don't be silly. Of course, I don't think you're a dog thief. But I am accusing you of lying to me."

Standing up, Jarrod brushed off his pants and approached Toya. "When have I ever lied to you, Ms. Toya?"

Folding her arms around her chest, she said, "When you came over here talking about Princess was your dog, but you needed someone to keep her for a little while. When the whole time you knew that you had bought her for me."

Jarrod opened his mouth to deny her claim, but the church kid in him caught up to his mouth, reminding him as his father had said many times, 'a liar can't tarry in God's eyesight.' So instead of lying, he asked, "You mad?"

She unfolded her arms. "I'm not mad. I know why you did it. And to be honest, I'm blessed to have you in my life. Because having Princess was probably exactly what I needed."

Jarrod smiled but didn't say anything.

"I don't even think I would have dared to leave my house to visit with Tia and Jayden last night if it hadn't been for the fact that Princess takes me out of the house about four times a day." Toya sat down next to Princess and rubbed her belly. "Each day, this dog has been building my confidence, and I hadn't even realized it."

"Does that mean you're going to keep her?"

"I'm not going that far? I need to get back to work sometime soon, and I don't see how I can manage Princess and a job with all her bathroom breaks."

Laughing, Jarrod told her, "We can train her to go out less, and if you get a house and a fence, she can go in your back yard."

"Sounds like you need to take your own advice. So, make sure your next place is a house with a fence, and you and I can share custody of *our* dog."

~~~

Princess needed a bath really bad. But Toya wasn't feeling the whole let-the-dog-bathe-in-the-tub thing, so she called a groomer and made an appointment. Then she called Jarrod to see if he wanted to take the dog for her.

"I wish I could, Toya. But I already made plans for this evening."

She wanted to ask if his plans included a woman, but that was none of her business. "You know what, Jarrod. Princess and I don't need you for this. I'll take her myself."

"Why don't you just switch the appointment to a different day, I know you don't like being out like that."

"Didn't I just spend the night with Tia. And I didn't have not one panic attack going or coming back home. I've got this."

"I'm proud of you, Toya. I knew you wouldn't let him win."

Toya smiled at that. "I'm kind of proud of me too." She hung up the phone, jumped in the shower, then put on a flowery sundress, and brushed her hair into a ponytail.

"Come on, Princess. It's time to get you a bath or a shower." She really didn't know how dog groomers washed dogs. They never had a dog when she was a kid, and she never wanted one in all the years that she had her own place. But there was something about Princess.

From the moment Princess rubbed her head against Toya's pants, she was in love.

Her dog had gotten her out of her cocoon. She was no longer content with being a hermit, she was ready to move on with her life. Maybe she'd even go to the mall or stop at the grocery store while Princess got herself all pretty and smelling good.

When they arrived at the groomers and discovered that Princess was fifth on the list and she had an hour and a half to kill, Toya got back in her car prepared to hang out while waiting on Princess. But when she drove up to the mall and watched all the people walking around, she started hyperventilating as she wondered if Marvel was in one of those stores and if he would see her as she walked by.

"Calm down, just calm down. Nobody is after you. You are safe," she gave herself a pep talk as she drove away from the mall. The grocery store was out of the question, she just wasn't ready yet.

As she headed back to the dog groomer, she realized that her favorite Mexican restaurant was on this street. She pulled up in the parking lot, practically licking her lips. She had chickened out of going to the mall and had a mini panic attack, but Toya was still proud of herself for even trying. The next time it won't be so difficult. But for now, she was going to treat herself to some shrimp nachos with extra cheese sauce with beans and rice.

She called in her order and then waited in her car for ten minutes strolling through Facebook on her phone. Everybody else seemed to be living panic attack free, but she was willing to bet that none of her Facebook friends had been kidnapped at gunpoint and tied up while the man they hoped to build a future with plotted ways to kill them. So, it was none of their business why she didn't post about fabulous vacations or post pictures of food anymore. She just wasn't feeling it. Toya had thought about deactivating her account, but sometimes she enjoyed seeing pictures of old friends in the Bahamas or Hawaii and even in Italy. It gave her hope that someday soon, that she would be enjoying her life again too.

She walked into the restaurant and went to the pickup area. "Order for Toya," she said to the clerk standing behind the cash register.

"Nineteen ninety-nine, please."

Toya handed the clerk the money and received her bag of goodies. She was on her way out the door and back to the safety of her car when Jarrod walked into the restaurant with this gorgeous, high cheekbone, cream complexion woman with coal black hair that flowed down her back. And not one hair was out of place. The woman looked good standing next to Jarrod, in all his chocolate glory.

Toya felt inadequate with her flower dress and ponytail. She wished she could have just blended into the wallpaper, but no such luck as Jarrod's eyes seemed to buck as he saw her.

"Hey, what are you doing here? I thought you had plans tonight?" That was stupid, Toya thought to herself. Of course, he had plans, and they were obviously with the woman who was now pulling on his elbow.

"Oh yeah." He looked uncomfortable as he glanced from the woman standing next to him, and then back at Toya. "Um, this is Lisa."

Lisa held out a hand to Toya. "I'm Toya," she said to the woman since Jarrod had obviously forgotten her name.

He jerked forward as if being pushed and put a hand on Toya's shoulder. "Lisa, this is Toya. She and I go way back."

Toya didn't understand why Jarrod felt the need to introduce her after she had already introduced herself. Or why he was standing there looking goofy. She lifted her bag, then said, "Well, I'll see you later."

"He-he-he,"

Jarrod did this stupid sounding laugh. Toya looked at him as if he had lost his mind. "Bye."

A couple seconds went by… "Of course, I'll see you later. We co-parent a dog, remember," Jarrod responded as if he was on some type of delay.

Toya kept walking and refused to look back. She knew she was being mean, but she hoped the girl would cheat on him and make him look silly for chasing after some beauty pageant chick, rather than going out with normal women, like her. Someone who wasn't afraid to come out of the house wearing a ponytail.

~~~

"Why do you seem a thousand miles away?" Lisa asked Jarrod as they ate their meal.

Jarrod looked down at his plate. He had been swirling the fork in the plate. His burrito was still untouched, and that wasn't like him. He loved Mexican food almost as much as Toya did. And the chicken burrito from this place was always banging.

He looked over at Lisa's plate. She had already eaten one of her three shrimp tacos. "Is it good?"

"Delicious. You were right about this place. I just don't understand why you haven't eaten any of your food yet. And why you keep looking back at the door like you think your friend," she lifted her fingers and put the word friend, in quotation marks, "is going to walk back in."

"Toya is my friend. But look, Lisa, I apologize if I've been distracted. You asked me to hang out with you this evening, and I owe you my undivided attention."

Lisa had a fork full of Spanish rice headed toward her mouth. She dropped the fork, letting it fall back onto her plate. "Oh, heck-to-the-naw, I don't need a pity date. So, let's get this straight, if another woman is on your mind while you're sitting here with me, we might as well end this date now."

Jarrod didn't consider this a date, just two people hanging out. Lisa was beautiful, most men would be thrilled to have her on their arm. But he just wasn't into her like that. He wished he was because things would be a lot less complicated in his life.

"I'm sorry about this, Lisa. I truly thought you just wanted to hang out with an old friend tonight. I didn't know you wanted this to lead to more than the friendship that we have."

In a huff, Lisa told him, "We don't have a friendship, Jarrod. Not if you can treat me like this. I think I'd better go."

"You don't have to do that, Lisa. Let's just finish our food, and I'll take you home."

She shook her head. "I don't want you to take me home. I feel like a fool as it is. I'll call someone to pick me up." The waitress stopped at the table to check on them, Lisa told her, "you can box our meals. Then she lifted out of her seat and headed toward the bathroom.

He really needed to stick with hanging out with the fellas, because his friendships with women always seemed to end badly. But no matter how upset Lisa was with him, he was not about to let her call an Uber. She would have to tolerate him for a few more minutes so he could see her home safely. But when she came out of the bathroom, Jarrod noticed that Lisa had freshened her make-up and lipstick.

She had a smug look on her face as she said, "You're excused."

Jarrod sat across from her dumbfounded. Did he hear her correctly? Did this woman just dismiss him after he sat at this table waiting on her to come out of that bathroom for twenty minutes?

"Are you a slow learner or what? I don't need you here anymore."

"I just want to take you home, Lisa. I am truly sorry if I upset you, but there is no need to ruin our friendship."

She shewed him away with the back of her hand. "Just go already. I have a ride."

"I don't want you taking an Uber. You don't have to do that." Her lips pursed as she crossed her eyes. "Okay, yeah, I was a bit distracted…"

She cut him off. "I don't do distracted men." she then stood up with this grin on her face.

Jarrod turned to see who she was smiling at. The former linebacker for the Detroit Lions had just walked into the restaurant. Lisa stretched out her arms to him as he stepped into her embrace.

"Hey babe, I'm glad you called." He said.

"I'm glad you were available for little ol' me," she purred.

"Always, baby. You know that."

Lisa touched the linebacker's big muscular arm, squeezed it and cooed.

"Who's your friend?" The guy asked as he looked at Jarrod.

Jarrod shook the man's hand and was about to introduce himself when Lisa said, "Who, him." She pointed at Jarrod and then smirk. "He's nobody." She pulled the man away from the table and then strutted out of the restaurant.

"I guess she showed me," Jarrod said to himself and then laughed his head off once he got into his car and headed home.

"Women are a trip." He shook his head and kept right on laughing about the situation.

8

Toya was lounging around at home on Saturday morning, still steaming over seeing Jarrod with that Ms. America chick when Gina called. She kind of felt guilty because she hadn't called Gina since they exchanged numbers and there was no reason for that because Toya wasn't busy at all. She was trying to think of an excuse for her behavior, but Gina took the conversation in another direction.

"How come you didn't tell me about the Armor of God Bible study at your mother's church?"

"I didn't know anything about it," Toya responded honestly. And then she wondered why she didn't know… and why hadn't her mother called her lately? They normally talked a few times a week, but Toya couldn't remember the last time she had hung out with her mother, let alone talked on the phone more than a minute or two.

"It really sounds like something I want to attend, but I didn't want to go by myself. Are you interested?"

She wanted to say no. Bible study had been her life since the day she was born, what more could she learn? But what else did she have to do? Also, the fact the Bible study was at her mother's church with people she had known for most of her life, was the other thing that made Toya say, "Sure, why not." If nothing else, she would go to church and find out why her mother has been too busy to talk to her.

The Bible study started at eleven in the morning, and Toya discovered that it wasn't a one-day event, but a seven-week Bible study that was being conducted like a webinar with Priscilla Shirer. Ever since watching Priscilla Shirer in the movie War Room, Toya had been a fan. But it wasn't like Priscilla was right here in the sanctuary leading this Bible study and she would be able to chat with her or even get an autograph at the end of the discussion. They were doing this Bible study via the eighty-inch screen that hung on the wall behind the pulpit in the sanctuary.

This screen was normally used on Sunday morning to project the scriptures that her mom or Thomas read from to deliver their message. Toya had no doubt that she would enjoy this Bible study, she didn't even mind that Priscilla was on the big screen rather than actually, in the flesh, standing behind the pulpit. But she couldn't see herself attending all seven Bible studies. So, she decided to just lean back in her seat, open her heart and mind and prepare herself to listen and take in everything this woman had to say. Since this might be the only study on the Armor of God that she would be attending.

But from the moment the video started, until it ended, Toya was mesmerized. The Bible study was based on Ephesians 6:10-19.

Finally, my brethren, be strong in the Lord and in the power of His might. Put on the whole armor of God, that you may be able to stand against the wiles of the devil.

For we do not wrestle against flesh and blood, but against principalities, against powers, against the rulers of the darkness of this age, against spiritual hosts of wickedness in the heavenly places.

Therefore, take up the whole armor of God, that you may be able to withstand in the evil day, and having done all, to stand. Stand therefore, having girded your waist with truth, having put on the breastplate of righteousness, and having shod your feet with the preparation of the gospel of peace; above all, taking the shield of faith with which you will be able to quench all the fiery darts of the wicked one.

And take the helmet of salvation, and the sword of the Spirit, which is the word of God; praying always with all prayer and supplication in the Spirit, being watchful to this end with all perseverance and supplication for all the saints— and for me, that utterance may be given to me, that I may open my mouth boldly to make known the mystery of the gospel.

Of course, Toya knew these scriptures, but she had never applied them to her life in any real and meaningful way. As far as Toya was concerned, Marvel was her enemy, and she needed to hide away from anything that looked like it might cause her the same kind of pain Marvel had tried to inflict on her. But according to Priscilla, mere mortal men and women weren't the problem.

The problem was that no matter who you are, or how spiritual you are, you are still in a wrestling match against the devil. But the devil is so cunning and deceitful that he tries to get us to fight against each other, the people and things we can see, rather than take on the real battle… the spiritual battle.

By the time the video ended, Toya could honestly say she had gained knowledge and wanted to hear more. The lights came back on in the sanctuary, and Pastor Yvonne was now standing behind the pulpit. She looked out at the crowd and said, "I want to thank each and every one of you for coming out to this event that our women's ministry diligently planned. As you were told at the beginning, this is a seven-session Bible study.

"I pray that you will join us for the next six weeks so that we can receive a clear understanding of how to put on this armor to withstand all the wiles of the evil one. If you've already purchased your companion book for this Bible study, we have them waiting on you in the fellowship hall. If you still need to purchase your book, please go to the church bookstore and take care of that. We will take questions next week after you've read week one's study in the Armor of God book."

With that said, her mother stepped down and walked directly to the spot where Toya and Gina were sitting. "Well, I see that the dynamic duo is back in business."

Gina stood and hugged Pastor Yvonne. "I wondered if you would remember me."

"How could I forget. You, Toya and Jarrod were inseparable in middle and high school." Yvonne stepped back a bit and gave Gina a good once over. "And you're just as beautiful as ever."

"Thank you, Pastor Yvonne. You are quite beautiful yourself."

"That's what my handsome husband tells me. But I can't get enough of hearing it." The two women laughed.

"Oh, congratulations on your new marriage. I was very sorry to hear about Pastor Milner's passing."

There was still that hint of sadness that is carried for our loved ones who have gone before us trying to bring her down, but the joy of new love blocked the sadness and enabled her to smile again. "Thank you, hon. Now, let me speak to this daughter of mine."

"I need to purchase my book for the Bible study anyway, so I'll get out of your way." Gina headed towards the back of the church where the bookstore was.

Yvonne sat down next to Toya and gave her daughter a big ol, I'm-so-glad-to-see-you-in-the-house-of-the-Lord hug. "Well, this is a pleasant surprise."

"It wouldn't be if you had picked up the phone and told me about the Bible study. I mean, really, Mom. I had to hear about this whole big elaborately planned event from Gina. And she hasn't even been back in town but a month and already she knows more about what's going on at my church than I do."

Yvonne looked at her oldest daughter, she hesitated, but only for a moment. "Honestly Toya, I didn't realize you still considered Christ-Life your church because you haven't stepped foot in here in about six months."

That was harsh. She hadn't been attending church, but only because she didn't like being out of the house and vulnerable. But her mother was acting like she had lost her religion and was now some Buddhist or something.

"Don't look at me like that. I'm not trying to hurt your feelings. I was just explaining why I didn't tell you about this event."

Toya stood when Gina came back into the sanctuary. "Well, just so you know, I enjoyed the Bible study, and I will be here for the entire study."

As Toya walked away from Yvonne, Thomas sat down and put an arm around his wife's shoulder.

"Did you hear that?" Yvonne asked.

"Yep, and I'm just thankful that prayer works. We stepped back and allowed God to move Toya forward, and we will soon rejoice as He finishes the work. I can promise you that."

"I must admit it was so hard for me to step back. You don't know how many times I wanted to pick up the phone and beg Toya to come back to church."

"She would have just made some excuse. God knew what she needed, and one day, I hope she will tell us all about it."

"Amen to that."

9

The second Bible study lesson dealt with the belt of truth. Priscilla Shirer's message was taken from Ephesians 6:13-14.

Therefore, take up the whole armor of God, that you may be able to withstand in the evil day, and having done all, to stand. Stand therefore, having girded your waist with truth.

Toya and Gina sat mesmerized by the word they were hearing. They were absolutely captivated because they had been attending church most of their life and had never had this thing broken down the way it was being broken down to them.

After the lesson, Toya and Gina grabbed a cup of coffee and a pastry that the church had laid out for the women attending the Bible study. They then sat down in the fellowship hall to digest all that they had taken in that morning. "What a word, what a word, what a word," was all Toya kept saying as she shook her head in disbelief.

"Who you telling. This building should be on fire because it was hot in there." Gina was just as amazed as Toya.

"I've been in church all my life, heard ministers preach on the belt of truth, but I've never heard anything explained the way Priscilla broke it down. But I'll tell you what, from this day on I'm going to stand firm in the truth of God."

When Toya finished speaking, Mother Thornton walked over to her table. She was the kindest woman Toya had ever known, and she loved the anointing that was on this woman. Toya stood and hugged her. "I didn't know you were here today. It is so good to see you."

"I saw you. This week and last week. You seem to truly be getting something from the Lord Himself, so I didn't want to disturb you. But I came over to let you know that God hasn't released me from my assignment yet so I'm still praying for you, Chile."

"Thank you, Mother Thornton." She hugged the woman again then pointed toward Gina. "Do you remember Gina? She used to attend this church years ago."

Mother Thornton turned toward Gina, and her eyes lit up. "Oh my God in heaven. I feel like Simeon when he saw the baby, Jesus. The Lord has allowed me to live long enough to see an answer to my prayers."

"Excuse me," Gina had a look of confusion on her face.

"Chile, your mama came to me years ago and asked me to pray you back home. She missed you so."

With tears in her eyes, Gina stood and hugged the kind old woman as well. "Thank you so much for praying for me. You'll never know how much that means to me."

The woman stepped back, looked Gina indirectly in the eye. "I know... the Lord has shown me the kind of trouble you and Toya are in. But I'm here to tell you that He is yet delivering. Stand still and see the salvation of the Lord." She pointed from Toya to Gina and back again. "Do you hear what I'm telling you?"

"Yes ma'am, I hear you," Toya said, and Gina co-signed.

When they sat back down, Gina appeared to be mulling something over. She wiped the tears from her face, then leaned a little closer to Toya. "Can I tell you something?"

"Of course, girl. You know you can tell me anything."

Gina nodded. "The reason I moved out of the country was to hide from this crazy man I used to date. I feared that if I ever came home, I could possibly lead him to my parents, and he might just kill them to get back at me."

Toya was totally caught off guard by that comment. She and her best friend had been apart for so many years, but it seems as if they had been living parallel lives. "Is that why you moved into our gated community, you still don't feel safe, do you?"

Gina lowered her eyes and shook her head. "He took that away from me. But my father got sick a few months back."

"Oh wow, I'm sorry to hear that."

Gina lifted a hand. "He's doing better now. But that's what finally convinced me to come back home. Finding our gated community was heaven sent for me. I didn't have to live with my parents and worry about my ex, the maniac coming to the house, but I'm still able to spend time with them."

"Family is important. We should never let anyone pull us away from the people who love and care for us the most." Toya was saying that to herself, just as much as she was saying it to Gina. She had almost allowed Marvel to do the same thing to her. Who knows, if Jarrod hadn't been in her life, bringing Princess when he did, she might have moved out of the country to escape the torment of constantly looking over her shoulder.

"Friends are important too," Gina said as if she had been reading Toya's thoughts.

Toya was in total agreement, she was just about to tell Gina about the man who almost drove her away from her friends and family when the door to the fellowship hall opened, and Jarrod walked in. As if she had been caught doing something wrong, Toya jumped out of her seat.

"There you are," Jarrod said, as he walked toward her.

"What are you doing here?" Toya asked.

"I'm meeting up with dad. He told me that you were here." Jarrod's eyes drifted to the right, and that's when he saw her. "Gina? Is that you?"

"Why do you sound so surprised? Didn't Toya tell you that I live in her community now?"

Pointing towards Gina, Jarrod turned back to Toya. "Is she the neighbor you bumped into while walking Princess a few weeks ago?"

"That would be me," Gina stood up and gave Jarrod a hug. "It's good to see you after all these years."

Toya still hadn't said a word. She was too busy trying to figure a way of explaining how she conveniently forgot to mention that Gina was back in town and living the next street over from her. Would he believe that it just totally slipped her mind? Should she be concerned that she was standing in the fellowship hall of her church trying to think of a lie? 'Jesus, help me,' she silently prayed.

Gina and Jarrod both sat down at the table. Toya joined them, right away, she started feeling like a third wheel as Jarrod suddenly became interested in Gina's life and what she had been doing for the past ten years.

When she couldn't take no more of Jarrod's obvious drooling over beautiful Gina, Toya put her purse on her shoulder and stood back up. "I'm going to let you two catch up. I'm sure Princess is missing me, so I'm heading home." Toya wanted to clamp her mouth shut, who admits out loud that they have no one in their life but a dog? As soon as those words were out of her mouth, she felt like she was back to being that teenage girl, sitting at home waiting on Jarrod to show up and take her to the prom.

"What was that about?" Jarrod asked as he followed Toya to her car.

Taking her keys out of her purse, she turned off the alarm and unlocked the door. "What are you talking about? And why did you follow me out here, I thought you were so interested in what Gina had to say?"

"Of course, I'm interested in what Gina has to say, I haven't seen her in ten years."

"Okay, so I got out of the way so you could talk to your ex-girlfriend. No big deal." She got in her car, but before she could close it, Jarrod wedges his body between her and the door.

"You're right, it's no big deal because Gina and I aren't a thing. But I am glad that I saw her today because I owe her an apology. I'm going to go back in church and give it to her."

"Go then, ain't nobody stopping you. But you are stopping me from driving off. I really do need to get home to Princess."

"I just want to make sure you understand that I don't want to date Gina. I know what I did in college changed the friendship that you and I had, and I don't ever want to experience that again." He walked away from her car, leaving her looking confused and conflicted.

He didn't have time to explain anything further to Toya. He meant what he said about apologizing to Gina. It was long past due, and he wasn't going to let Toya stop him from handling his business.

As Jarrod re-entered the church, Gina was at the trash can throwing away her coffee cup. She smiled at him as he approached. "I thought you left with Toya. I was about to get going myself."

"No, I didn't want to leave before talking with you." He pointed towards the table they had been sitting at before Toya left. "Would you mind sitting back down with me for a minute?"

"For an old friend like you, how can I say no." Gina sat back down.

"I'm glad you still consider me a friend because that's what I want to talk to you about."

Putting her elbow on the table, she then put her hand under her chin. "I'm all ears," she told him, with a hint of mischievousness in her voice.

He pulled out a chair and sat down next to her. "Before we begin, I want you to know I was so happy to see you today because for years I've wanted to apologize to you."

"Wait... what are you apologizing for? You didn't do anything to me."

"I let you down. My pride got in the way, and I couldn't face you after I came back from Christmas break that year. I stopped speaking to you for something that wasn't your fault, and even when you started dating that dude that I knew was all wrong for you, I never said a word."

"Larry Williams," Gina said as she strolled back down memory lane. "He was a player, but so were you back then."

"Yeah, but I knew you deserved better."

"To be honest with you, Larry was much better than the guy I started dating after college. The man after Larry was mean and violent. I ended up in the hospital with a broken arm after one of his abusive episodes."

"I'm so sorry that happened to you. That just makes me feel even worse, because if you and I had stayed friends, maybe I would have been able to steer you away from a man like that."

"It was not your fault, Jarrod. You were probably the best guy I ever went out with. It was just too bad that you were hung up on Toya. But also, it seems like the kind of luck I have with men, which is why I've given up dating altogether."

"I hate hearing that, as beautiful as you are, inside and out, you deserve to have a man who adores you."

"God knows what's best for me, so if I am to remain single, then that's the way it will be. I guarantee you, God Himself will have to tell me that the next man I allow in my life is from Him or I'm not falling for it."

Jarrod laughed at that. "Well, that's why the Bible says that the man who finds a wife, finds a good thing and obtains favor from the Lord. So, believe me, he will find you."

"That sounds scary to me."

"Not scary at all if it's the right person."

"Speaking of that." Gina scooted a little closer to Jarrod. She looked around to make sure there was no one within earshot. "What happened with you and Toya? Why didn't you ever tell her how you felt back then?"

"This is the reason I stopped speaking to you because I didn't want to answer this exact question. Now, do you want me to walk away again?" He said it playfully, but his eyes still held a tinge of pain from what could have been.

Gina nudged his shoulder. "You want me to accept your apology, then fess up."

He took his arm and acted like he was twisting it behind his back. "Okay, stop twisting. Let's just say Toya was unavailable that year. So, I felt like I missed my moment and came back to college without saying anything to her."

"Well, she sure is available now."

"I'm not so sure about that," Jarrod said as he and Gina stood up. He hugged her and watched her leave, then he tried to pull himself together before he met up with his father. But seeing Gina had brought all those teenage feelings back in full force. But it wasn't the friendship kind of love he had for Gina that was bothering him. It was the man-finds-a-wife kind of love he had for Toya that grabbed hold of him his junior year of college and hadn't loosened its grip. What he was supposed to do with that, Jarrod just didn't know.

10

After Toya walked Princess, she wasn't feeling much like staying at home. Her mother was always busy with church activities, so she hesitated to call her. But then she realized that Tia couldn't hang out like she used to, not now that she had the baby and she certainly wasn't calling Gina. So, she picked up the phone and called her mother. To her surprise, her mother was available, so they met at one of their favorite soul food restaurants for a late lunch.

"Thanks for hanging out with me, Mom. I really didn't feel like sitting around the house doing nothing today."

"I'm so glad to hear that, because to tell you the truth, Thomas and I have been a bit worried that you were becoming too reclusive."

Toya hadn't thought that anyone was paying attention to her struggles. "Why didn't you say anything?"

"We've been praying for you."

"Thank you for that." The waitress brought their food to the table. Her mother said grace and then Toya admitted, "I didn't want to worry you. I felt bad enough about not listening to you when you told me not to date Marvel."

Yvonne put a hand over Toya's. "You can come to me with anything, you know that, don't you?"

Toya nodded. "I just didn't understand what was happening to me when I first started having panic attacks every time I left work. But now I know that I was subconsciously reliving the day Marvel kidnapped me from work."

"You never even told me you were having panic attacks. That's not something I should just now be hearing. But I am glad that you were able to figure out what was triggering them?"

"This Armor of God Bible study has really been helping me deal with things that have been troubling me and figure out who the true enemy is. Now I know I'm in a battle and I'm fighting it with God's help."

"I'm so glad that this Bible study is ministering to you."

"It is. I just wish you had done this study a few months ago, maybe I wouldn't have quit my job."

"You'll find another job. My strong, vibrant daughter is beginning to emerge again, and nothing is going to stop you. I'm proud of who you are becoming."

"Me too. But in truth, Jarrod had a lot to do with that as well."

"I heard that you've fallen in love."

Toya's cheeks reddened as her eyes widened. "Mom, Jarrod, and I are not in love. We are friends... always have been. I mean, Jarrod isn't interested in me like that anyway."

Yvonne leaned back in her chair and studied her daughter. "I wasn't talking about you and Jarrod. I was talking about Princess."

"Oh, yes, of course, you were talking about Princess. That dog has helped me more than you know. I'm out here having lunch with you and haven't had a panic attack in weeks. All that dog walking broke me of those panic attacks."

Yvonne smiled. "You think it was the dog walking... I think it was all the praying Thomas and I have been doing."

They took a break from talking as they dug into the mac and cheese, yams, fried chicken, and delicious cornbread. Even though they were enjoying the meal, Toya admitted, "I've got to start back eating right, I have put on ten more pounds in the last few months."

"This is definitely not an everyday thing for me. So, I'm going to enjoy every bit of this fried chicken," Yvonne told her as she picked up a napkin and wiped the grease from her fingers.

"You can eat whatever you want because you never gain weight anyway. Thomas is a blessed man to have a wife like you."

"That's what he tells me." Now it was Yvonne's turn to blush. "But what about you, sweetheart? Are you ready to give love another try?"

Toya didn't even know how to answer that. There had only been one man that she had wanted to spend forever with. But he didn't feel the same way, so she just had to make the best of the loveless life she had.

~~~

"So, what's our plan for today, old man?" Jarrod enjoyed reminding his father about his age, especially since the elder Reed's fountain of youth tree had obviously shaved twenty years off the man; he didn't look a day over fifty, and he was almost seventy.

"I got your old man. Just let me get you back on that court. I'll show you who's the old man and who still has hops."

"Oh no you don't. I'm not about to be the cause of your heart attack. You are not allowed on the basketball court with me or anyone else. Don't make me tell Yvonne about the last time." There was no quit in his father. He wasn't going to lose gracefully and would fight to the bitter end. The last time they shot hoops, his dad worked up such a sweat that he almost dehydrated himself.

"I beat you that last time and the time before that if I recall correctly," Thomas said, getting up from behind his desk and putting on his suit jacket.

"Yeah, yeah, yeah, you're the man. Alright, you don't have to prove yourself to me or anyone else. I mean it, dad. You scared me."

Looking guilty as charged, he admitted, "I did overdo it. But that's only because you provoked me."

"Well, I'm good for hanging out, just as long as there's no sports involved. I get it already. You are better than me in basketball... that's why you had to pay for all my college fees. If you had made sure I had skills, I could have gotten myself a basketball scholarship. Maybe even gone pro."

"Look at you, dreaming big." Thomas nudged his son toward the door. "I'd say you turned out alright, even better than some of those guys who went pro. Because I guarantee you not many of them have the heart for people that you have."

"I wouldn't mind a few extra dollars along with my heart."

"Who wouldn't, son... who wouldn't." They walked out of the church and got in Thomas's SUV. "I'm doing my hospital visits today, and I wanted some company. You up for it?"

"Well, since you didn't tell me until you had me in the car and locked the doors, I guess I'd better go."

"You can always say no. I just thought you'd like to see Mrs. Brown."

"Deacon Brown's wife?" When Thomas nodded, Jarrod said, "So you did help with her medical bills?"

"Ethel is a good woman. She had been attending the church for three decades with her husband. Of course, we helped her."

"How is Mrs. Ethel doing?"

"She had heart surgery a few weeks ago. They had to replace valves because they were so blocked that she could have died at any moment. But she has been steadily improving since the surgery. I believe she will be going home this week."

"I'm so glad y'all were able to help her, especially since she will be going home without her husband."

"From what the prosecutor told me; Brown is looking at least three to five years. But Ethel has three daughters, and one of them has moved back home to help her during her time of recovery."

"Good. But with Mrs. Ethel's health condition, you can kind of understand how Deacon Brown became so desperate."

Thomas didn't agree with that. "Brown didn't have to steal from the church or shoot himself to get our help. It was his pride that wouldn't let him verbalize his needs. He could have received help the right way."

"I know about that pride stuff, Dad. I think it has cost me the one woman I truly want to be with."

"Toya." It was a statement, not a question.

Jarrod's head jerked toward his father. "You knew?"

"I've known for a long time, Son. What I couldn't figure out though, was how you messed up the prom thing."

Jarrod pounded his skull with his fist and then shook his head as if he was trying to rattle it free or something. "She won't let me live down that one dumb mistake, Dad. It's not like Toya is so perfect. She has made mistakes too."

"Yeah, but Toya was the one who asked you to the prom. You had her right where you wanted her. All you had to do was take her to prom and then tell her how you felt. But you chose to stand her up. I never said anything to you about it, but you hurt her that day."

"I was young. I was confused." His hands went to his face again. But this time he wasn't trying to pound some sense into it, he used his open palm to massage his temples. He took a deep breath. "When Toya, Gina and I were planning which college we would attend. I told her that I wanted to attend Howard University.

"Gina and I both put in our applications to Howard. I thought Toya did too. But she never confirmed. Then, a couple of weeks before the prom, she tells me that she has been accepted at Stanford. She wouldn't even give me an explanation for why she didn't apply at Howard like I thought she was going to do."

Thomas glanced over at Jarrod as they pulled up to a red light. "I thought you knew."

Jarrod shook his head. "Knew what?"

"David graduated from Stanford. Toya probably picked that school to honor her father."

Sighing, Jarrod said, "I guess I can understand that. But what made me so mad at the time was that the three of us filled out the application for Howard University together, but Toya never planned to attend in the first place. She should have just told me. And then I started thinking about how far away she would be for so many years, and I just didn't see any reason why we should go to the prom and look into each other's eyes on that dance floor. Possibly kiss, and then I would be left to think about that while she partied it up in California… at least, that's the way my eighteen-year-old self saw the matter."

"And now?"

"Now, I realize how fast time can pass. Now I realize the second chances don't come so easy."

11

When Toya arrived home, she went into her office, sat down in front of her computer, and began sending out resumes. It was time for her to get back to work, enough of this foolishness. The armor of God protected her, so she didn't have to be afraid.

She pulled up her resume to look over it one more time before sending it out. As she read through it, she noticed that she still had information about being the editor of her college newspaper. It wasn't like she had received any awards for her stellar reporting, and she had no interest in becoming a reporter, so it was time to remove this information from her resume.

Even as she deleted the entry, Toya smiled at the memory of being a writer on the same newspaper that her father had once served as editor. That probably had something to do with them, allowing her on the paper in the first place.

Feeling a bit melancholy as she thought of her father, Toya got down on the floor in her office. She pulled one of the four boxes over to her. The boxes had been cluttering her office, waiting to be opened so she could get her home office organized. She wasn't in the mood to open the box with pictures, vases, and sculptures that would add the official office look to this room. No, the box she opened was full of memories. It held some of the articles she wrote on her school newspaper and some days, when she was thinking about her dad and feeling sad, she read those articles out loud as if she were reading them to him.

"What's this?" She picked the packet up, opened it, and put the contents on her desk. "Wow, am I a pack rat or what?" She was staring at not just one, but two of her college acceptance letters.

Toya looked heavenward as she thought about her beloved father. The man who took her to her first dance, who bandaged her knee when she bruised it and who made her and Tia feel like he loved them more than anything or anyone. She looked at the wall directly in front of her desk where her Stanford University degree hung. Toya still remembered the day she made the decision to attend…

Toya, girl, get down here and eat some breakfast. You do not want to take your exams on an empty stomach, I can promise you that." Her father yelled up the stairs.

"Dad, I don't have time to eat breakfast. And besides, mom is out of town, preaching somewhere."

"I made breakfast, now get down here."

Her father was no cook. She wished he would stop trying. But with her mother's popularity growing on the preaching circuit, he had been standing in as the house cook a couple times a week lately. Why didn't he just order in or take them out for breakfast and dinner? That would be better than eating the weird concoctions he came up with.

One morning he actually thought that she and Tia would eat lumpy grits and baloney sandwiches for breakfast. Then later that night, he came up with bacon sandwiches and jello. Why was he torturing himself and his daughters? Toya was just going to tell him to stick to the things he was good at and order pizza for dinner.

But when she stepped into the kitchen and found a table spread with eggs, pancakes, bacon, sausage and hash browns, she said, "Did you hire a cook?"

"No silly, your mom got back home late last night. We are celebrating this morning, she wouldn't miss this for the world."

"Oh really, what exactly are we celebrating?"

"Just hold on, eat your breakfast. Your mom will be back in the kitchen, and we will let both of you know what's going on."

"Dig in, Toya. The food is really good this morning," Tia told her.

Toya filled her plate as she wondered what could be so important that her mother would get on a plane after preaching so that she could be home this morning. She normally didn't come back home until the day after her speaking engagement.

Yvonne Milner strutted into the kitchen wearing a long flowing house gown, her mother was beautiful and regal all in one. There was an envelope in both her hands, she laid them in front of Toya and stood back. "Your dad told me what arrived in the mail yesterday and I begged him not to open them with you until I was here. I hope you're not too mad about waiting an extra day."

Toya glanced down at the envelopes in front of her. One was from Stanford University, and the other was from Howard. "They both came yesterday?"

Her dad looked a bit sheepish as he confessed, "The Howard University letter came about three days ago. Stanford arrived yesterday."

"I was wondering why I didn't receive a letter from Howard. Because Gina and Jarrod both have their acceptance letters already."

"I didn't want you to make a rash decision before knowing whether or not you were accepted at Stanford." Her Dad stood before her, eyes pleading for understanding. "It just would mean so much to me if you went to Stanford, like your old man."

"Well, we don't know if I was accepted to either school. So, let's just see what these letters say first, okay?" Toya didn't want to disappoint her father, but if Stanford rejected her, she could go to Howard with her friends, and that would be that.

She opened the Howard letter first. Gina and Jarrod got in. Her grades were as good as theirs, so she hoped that Howard was impressed with her application too. And they were. She read the letter to her parents, confirming that Howard wanted her too.

"Now open the other one," her father said.

That was the day that changed things for her and Jarrod. She'd never told Jarrod that she had been accepted to Howard as well as Stanford. What would have been the use? Her father had been so happy when he discovered that she had been accepted to his Alma Mater. She just couldn't take that joy away from him by deciding on another school.

Toya hadn't known what the future would hold for her father. She didn't know that he would pass away just a few years after she graduated, so in hindsight, she was glad she chose to keep that smile on her daddy's face for just a little while longer. She wouldn't trade anything for how emotional Pastor David Milner had been the day she walked across that platform and took hold of her degree.

Her decision to be the responsible one also freed Tia to announce to the family that she wasn't interested in college in the normal sense. She wanted to go to art school, and her parents said yes. Tia was thrilled to be able to drop out of college for art school, while

Toya graduated and then went on to law school as she was expected to... now, what was she supposed to do?

Her phone rang, taking her out of her musings. It was Tia. "Hey girl, I was just thinking about you. How is my beautiful niece?"

"She is so perfect, Toya. Some days I can't believe it myself. Mom always said that I was a fussy baby, so I keep waiting for her to do the same to me. You know how they say the same mess you dished out to your parents you get it back double with your kids."

"Yeah, I've heard that, but I hope it's not true."

"You and me, both sister."

Laughing at her, Toya said, "And you better not yell at Jayden when she does start giving you trouble. You always used to cry and say that mom was mean when she got upset with you."

"I know, I really gave that woman a hard time. I probably should send her some flowers or something."

"You owe Mom flowers for the next ten years," Toya told her, still laughing.

"Yeah, okay, we all know that you were the golden child that did everything right. But I'm grown now and making better choices whether you and mom believe it or not."

"Oh, I believe it, Tia. I can see how you've grown. It makes me proud to be your big sister."

"Don't make me cry. You'll make me forget why I called you in the first place."

"So, there's a reason for this call?"

"Yes, ma'am. You'll never guess who I saw at the grocery store this morning?"

"Who?"

"Don't you want to guess?"

"Did you just say that I'll never be able to guess? So, spill it. Who did you see?"

"Peter Gallagher."

"Who?"

"Are you an owl or something? You know Peter Gallagher. You dated him in college. For goodness sake, you brought him home to meet mom and dad during Christmas break one year."

Toya snapped her finger. "Oh yeah, I almost forgot about Peter. That man was so dull that I almost fell asleep every time I was around him."

"It didn't look that way when he came home with you for Christmas. You hung all over that man so bad I thought you were going to come home in the summer and announce a pregnancy."

"Shut up, Tia. I was not that bad."

"Oh yes you were, but not all the time. It was like you barely knew him when it was just the family at the house. But when company came to the house, you were suddenly in love or something."

Or something was certainly the case. Because Toya didn't even like Peter, let alone love him. He was pompous, arrogant, and a know it all. Toya broke up with him two minutes after they arrived back on campus. She never even looked back to wonder what he was doing with his life.

"He's the new Dean of Students over at Michigan State University in case you want to know."

"Thank you, if I'm ever in need of a dean, I will look him up," Toya said with much sarcasm in her voice. But when they hung up the phone, Toya realized something that shook her very core.

Gina told her that Jarrod had come home to confess his love for her during Christmas break junior year. Now she remembered clear as if it had happened yesterday when Jarrod called and told her he wanted to talk to her about something when he and his parents came over for Christmas Eve dinner. Toya had thought he was going to tell her that he and Gina were getting married or talk about how much he loved being with Gina and she just didn't want to hear it. That was the reason she asked Peter, the obnoxious one, to come home with her for Christmas.

Jarrod had taken one look at her all hugged up with Peter, and he left the house without having dinner. She thought he had better things to do, but maybe what she had done that year had hurt and confused him. Maybe she owed Jarrod an apology.

12

The day of reckoning had finally come. Toya was going to deal with whatever this thing was between her and Jarrod, and she was going to live with the outcome. First, she called Gina and apologized for her behavior the other day.

"No need for apologies, girl. You and Jarrod need to figure out what you're doing, so other people won't keep getting caught in the middle."

"You're right, I know you are. But I felt so foolish when he left me sitting in my living room with my prom dress on and no date."

"That's the past, Toya. Trust me when I tell you that Jarrod has a thing for you. Always has, and probably always will."

"But, I'm the one who asked him to prom. So, it stands to reason that he doesn't think of me like that, and that's the reason he didn't want to take me to the prom, right?"

Gina sighed, wishing her friend would just get this already. "I don't know why he didn't show up for your date way back in high school. But I do know what he confessed to me when we were in college. So, like I said, the two of you need to talk and leave the rest of us out of it."

Toya had done damage to her friendship with Gina. She constantly put Gina on the back burner whenever she perceived the slightest of infractions where Jarrod was concerned. But it was time to stop blaming Gina because things didn't turn out the way she had hoped. Anyway, she had never expressed her true feelings for Jarrod to Gina or anyone else for that matter. Toya had matured enough to own her faults and missteps.

"I promise you, right here and now that I will never let anything or anyone else come between our friendship."

"Good because I really need you in my life."

Toya heard the crack in Gina's voice and realized just how much pain the loss of their friendship has caused Gina. She would never hurt her friend again. "I need you too. I have truly missed you."

~~~

Now to deal with the real problem at hand. Jarrod was supposed to meet up with her to take Princess for the weekend. But she wasn't just going to let him waltz in and leave without finally being straight up with her.

"I'm on my way," Jarrod told her.

"I'll be here," she said. When she hung up the phone, she ran to her walk-in closet and hurriedly took off her Feed-Me-Coffee pajamas, jumped in the shower then threw on a white sundress that flowed all the way to the floor and made her look like an angel.

She looked in the mirror and shook her head. "Girl, you trying too hard." She took off the beautiful dress and threw on a pair of stonewashed jeans and a beige halter top. That way, if he played her a fool, at least she wouldn't have dressed up like she expected to be taken out to dinner. "What do you think, Princess? Will this work?"

The dog looked up at Toya and leaned her head to the right as if she was studying her. She then barked two times and walked out of the room.

"You don't have to be rude. You could have just let me know that you didn't like it. You didn't have to walk away like that." Toya took the halter top off and put on her loose-fitting denim shirt with a drawstring at the bottom.

The buzzer announced that there was someone at the gate. Looking through the camera positioned at the gate, she could see that it was Jarrod, so she buzzed him in. Then she ran to the bathroom and dab some blush on her cheeks, eyeliner around her eyelids and a little lip gloss. By the time the doorbell rang, she was ready for Jarrod.

"I'm coming," she yelled as Princess started barking.

She opened the door, the moment Princess saw Jarrod, she stopped barking and almost knocked him down as she pounced on him. "She's getting big."

"Tell me about it," Toya agreed. "I had no idea that German Shepherds grew so fast. She is slinging me around when I walk her now."

"Poor Toya. You need some more meat on your bones." Jarrod gave Princess a hug and ruffled her ears. "You got her stuff ready?"

"I sure do, but how are you planning to sneak this big dog into your apartment? One bark from Princess and your landlord will probably throw you out before you get a chance to move out."

With a sheepish, lopsided grin on his face, Jarrod admitted, "I moved to my new place this week."

Hand on hips, eyes shooting daggers. "And just when were you going to tell me?"

"I wasn't trying to keep it from you, Toya."

"Oh, yes, you were. You just don't want to take responsibility for Princess. I know you, Jarrod, you ain't slick as you think you are."

"I like sharing ownership with you. And Princess loves you so much. You can't tell me that you don't want her around anymore."

She took her hands off her hips as Princess rubbed up against her leg. She rubbed the dogs head, "I love you too, Princess." But then she turned back to Jarrod. "But sometimes I need a break. This dog is a lot of work."

"I got you, I'm taking her off your hands right now. You won't have to lift a finger or think about her all weekend long. Just give me her stuff, and we'll get out of your way."

She could trust Jarrod to do exactly what he said. He had always been like that. No matter what Toya needed, he would take care of it. Right now, she needed rest from her dog. But not before she received answers from this man that she had always been in the friend zone with.

"Can you sit down so I can talk to you about something before you leave and give me this weekend break that I so desperately need?"

He hesitated. "You aren't still tripping about Gina, are you?"

Toya shook her head. "I already apologized to Gina, and I want to apologize to you as well. My behavior was uncalled for."

He sat down. "Then I have all the time you need. What's on your mind, pretty lady?"

"Do you really think I'm pretty?" Butterflies fluttered in her stomach as she sat down next to him. 'Lord, please let him feel the same way I do.'"

"Have you looked in a mirror today, or any day for that matter. Of course, I think you're pretty... no, I take that back, you're not just pretty. You, Toya Milner, are downright gorgeous."

"Thanks for saying that."

"I'm not just trying to be nice. I really mean it, Toya. I've always thought that about you."

"Then why haven't you ever told me?"

Jarrod shrugged. "I don't know. I guess things just got in the way."

"What kind of things?"

His eyebrows scrunch as he gave her a questioning glance. "Why are you asking me all of this?"

She took a deep breath as she gathered her courage. "To be honest, Gina told me that during Christmas break our junior year, you came home to tell me how you felt about me. Is that true?"

"I should have known Gina would run her mouth."

"But is it true?" Toya needed to hear him say it. She needed to know she hadn't been in her feelings all these years alone.

"What does it matter? When I came to see you, you were all hugged up with some guy even though you knew I was coming through. You didn't want to hear anything I had to say."

"I'm sorry about that. I only asked Peter to come home with me after you told me you wanted to talk over Christmas break." A look of embarrassment crossed her face. "I thought you were going to tell me that you and Gina were in love and making future plans or something. I just couldn't bear to hear that from you."

"So, what was really going on with you and that guy?"

"Nothing, I couldn't stand being around him. Peter was so full of himself, even while we were in college and he hadn't accomplished anything yet."

Jarrod stared at Toya as if seeing her for the first time and then he burst out laughing.

"What's so funny?"

He kept laughing, even while saying, "I shouldn't be laughing, because it's not funny. It's not funny at all."

"Then stop laughing." She picked up one of the pillows from the sofa and cracked him upside the head with it.

"Okay, okay. Don't get violent." Jarrod grabbed the pillow, so she couldn't hit him with it again. "There, I stopped laughing." But then he started shaking his head as memories of those days flooded in. "Do you have any idea how miserable I was after seeing you with that guy?"

"Probably about as miserable as I was when I found out you and Gina were dating."

Wagging a finger back and forth, Jarrod told her, "You really can't call what Gina and I did dating. Every time we were together, all I did was talk about you. It was so bad that Gina finally called me out about it.

"I couldn't help it," he told her. "You were so far away, and I missed you so bad, I just wanted to be close to someone who I could share all the memories I had of you with." He shrugged again. "But it wasn't fair to Gina."

"Is that why you wanted to apologize to her last week?"

"It was a little more to it than that. You see, when I got back to school that year, I was destroyed. But I was also embarrassed that I had finally confessed my feelings for you to someone, and I still didn't have anything to show for it. I didn't want to tell Gina that you were in love with someone else, so I stopped talking to her.

"I was hanging out with other girls and completely ignoring her. That's when she got involved with this guy that I knew was all wrong for her. But I didn't feel like I could say anything because I was dating a bunch of women who were all wrong for me too."

"Now that I think about it, Gina must have been lonely for a very long time with both of us turning our backs on her. That wasn't fair."

"And that's why I apologized to her."

Smiling, Toya said, "I'm glad you didn't let my bad attitude stop you from going back into the church and doing that for Gina." Toya playfully punched him on the shoulder. "I'm really kind of proud of you."

"Now that we've got that straight," Jarrod inched closer to her. He put a hand on her back and let his hand drift from her shoulder blade to her lower back. "Let's talk about us." But instead of talking, Jarrod leaned forward and kissed her.

His lips were soft and moist and sensual at the same time. Heat rose from her feet all the way to the top of her head until she thought she would explode from the pure joy of being on the sofa, locked in an embrace with Jarrod.

13

"Wait a minute." Toya pushed him back. She had to keep her wits about her. No way was she going to let Jarrod run in and out of her life. She wasn't willing to give up their friendship if it only meant dating him for a few months and then being awkward with each other the rest of their lives. They would, after all, have to see one another since her mother was now married to his father.

"That kiss felt like heaven, why'd you push me away." He tried to pull her back into his arms. But she wasn't having it.

"I need a clear head to talk this out with you."

"You still want to talk?"

"More than ever now." She wasn't letting him weasel out of this.

Jarrod wallowed on the sofa like a man in misery.

"Are you done?" Toya was about to pinch him, but Jarrod straightened back up and looked her in the eye so that he was giving her his full attention.

"Now, what I don't understand is, if you have feelings for me, and had them way back when why did you stand me up for our prom?"

"Are we back on this again? Why can't anyone let this go?"

"Who else asked you about this?"

"My dad, just the other day he basically asked in the same way you just did."

"Well, what did you tell him?"

Looking a little frustrated by the matter, Jarrod gritted his teeth before saying, "I'm just going to lay it out there for you. And then you can do with it what you will."

"Why are you angry? I think I have a right to know why you stood me up, don't you?"

"I'm not angry at you, I'm angry at that stupid kid I used to be. He really messed things up for me." Shaking his head at the situation, Jarrod finally said, "Look, the truth of the matter is that I was hurt that you lied to me about sending that college application to Howard University when all the while you only had your eyes set on Stanford."

"Are you kidding? You really thought I lied about that?"

He nodded.

Toya got up and went into her office. When she came back into the living room, she was carrying two pieces of paper. She handed both of them to Jarrod. "God works in mysterious ways because I just found both of these letters the other day. Now I have proof that I'm not some liar as I've been accused of being.

"What's this?"

"Can you read or not?"

He looked down at the papers. His eyes trailing from one and then the other. When he looked back at her, Jarrod's eyes were filled with questions. "But you never said anything."

"I couldn't."

"But the Howard acceptance letter is dated three days before the Stanford letter. Why didn't you say anything when you received it?"

"My dad didn't give me the Howard letter until the Stanford letter had also arrived. He wanted me at Stanford. And I'm glad I didn't disappoint him."

"I'm sure Uncle Dave was thrilled to have you at his alma mater. I'm just sorry that I was such a jerk about it. I honestly don't even know what I was thinking. It was your life, and you should have been able to live it how you pleased. I should have supported your decision."

"Yes, you should have," Toya agreed.

He rushed back to the sofa, sat down next to her and took her hand in his. "Is it too late for us, Toya?" He closed his eyes, silently praying that he hadn't messed things up to the point of no repair.

"I don't know," she said slowly. "I mean, what about that woman I saw you out with last month? Are you a couple or what? Because I'm not trying to come in between anything."

"Are you talking about Lisa Sampson?"

"Is that the woman I saw you with when I took Princess to the vet?"

"Yes."

"Then you know that's who I'm asking about. Don't beat around the bush, Jarrod. Just tell me straight up what's going on. Because we both know you've been known to date several women at once."

"In the past, I have dated several women at once. I've haven't done anything like that in years. So, don't go labeling me a dog when I'm far from it."

"Okay then, I stand corrected. Now tell me about Lisa."

"Lisa and I used to be friends. But she's dating a football player now." Jarrod added, "and yeah, maybe if I wasn't already head over heels in love with another stubborn woman, maybe I would have been interested in Lisa, but I just wasn't. And she for sure isn't thinking about me."

"Who you calling stubborn." She objected, but she objected with this big silly grin on her face.

He touched the tip of her nose with his index finger. "You, that's who. What are you going to do about it?"

Balling her fists, she told him, "I've been known to fight, so don't mess with me."

He took hold of her fist and pulled her to him until they were nose to nose, then lips to lips.

When the kiss ended, Toya stared at him for what seemed like a thousand and one years as she tried to make sense out of what had just happened to her. She had never felt like this after a simple kiss. But Jarrod wasn't just some random guy. He was the one who had always been there for her. Their friendship meant everything to her. And at this moment she was scared out of her mind.

What if it didn't work out? What if Jarrod found someone he wanted more than he wanted her. Toya's heart would be broken, and she didn't know if she could handle that. "You'd better leave."

"What? Why? I thought we were still talking."

"You promised me a weekend to myself. You and Princess need to go hang. I need some time to think."

Jarrod stood, straightened his pants, and adjusted his shirt. "Okay, Ms. Toya, I'll get out of your way. But I'm not letting another ten years go by before we resolve this. I want to be with you and you alone. So, you need to make up your mind."

"It's not that simple, Jarrod. There is a lot we have to consider."

He shook his head. "What is going on right here and right now is between the two of us and no one else."

"But your dad is married to my mother. You and I are basically brother and sister. How can we just start dating?"

"My dad has nothing to do with this." He put his hands on her shoulder as he stood in front of her imploring her to hear him out. "I have been in love with you far longer than my dad and Yvonne have been in love. So, you're not going to tell me that their marriage cancels out what I feel for you. Because it just doesn't."

"But if things don't work between us, it will be awfully awkward during Thanksgiving dinners, not to mention Christmas or church."

He removed his hands from her shoulders. He couldn't bear to touch her any longer. Not when he didn't know where things stood. "I'll give you until Sunday evening when I bring Princess back to make up your mind."

"That's only two days, Jarrod. How can I possibly make a decision this important in just two days?"

There was a hint of pain in his eyes, but he was committed to his decision. "I'm not going to live the rest of my life wondering what might have been or what could be. Loving you has stopped me from having the life I've been dreaming about for far too long. So, this is it, Toya. Either we're going to have this beautiful life together, or I'm moving on."

~~~

"He actually said that," Gina asked.

Toya had her cell phone up to her ear as she complained about the unreasonable demands Jarrod was making on her. "I couldn't believe it. Jarrod knows that there is a lot at stake when two friends decide to get romantic. Look what happened to the two of you."

"It did take us ten years to speak to each other again. But that was different. Jarrod just didn't want the reminder of you. Anyway, what makes you think it won't work out?"

"I don't know if it will work out, that's what's so scary about this." Toya could hear the whine in her voice, and at that moment, she wondered if she was being insensitive to Gina. "Does this conversation bother you. After all, you and Jarrod did hook up."

"I wouldn't call it a hookup. I told you that Jarrod didn't want me. He wanted someone he could talk about you with... someone who would understand and laugh at all of our memories."

"I don't believe that was all there was to it. When you called and told me about the two of you, you sounded so excited."

"Yes, I had been excited. But I don't believe Jarrod was ever excited about the possibility of us. And believe me, I got over it quickly. I'm not carrying a torch for Jarrod, so you can talk this situation over with me, and I will try my best to help you see the truth."

"And what is the truth?"

"The man loves you. He's probably loved you since junior high school. And that's a really long time to love someone and not know if they love you back."

"Of course, I love Jarrod. How could I not?"

"Not just love him, Toya. He wants you to be in love with him. Can you do that for him, or if not, can you release him so that he can find someone who will love him?"

"That's silly. I don't have Jarrod stuck. He's a free man. He can do whatever he wants."

"Stop it, Toya. It's time for you to take a leap of faith. Can you do it?"

"What about you?" Toya tried to turn the table on her friend. "Why are you still single? Where is your faith?"

"Don't try to change the subject, girlfriend. This isn't about me, it's about you and Jarrod."

"But don't you want to be happy too?" Toya prodded.

"Put it this way, I gave love a try, and it blacked my eye. So, I'm sitting out for a while. You just don't know who you can trust out there. I'm safer alone than with some man I don't know anything about," Gina said matter-of-factly.

Toya was sorry that she caused Gina to think about the awful experience she'd had with a man she loved. Domestic violence was a terrible thing. But so was being kidnapped at gunpoint. But none of that had anything to do with Jarrod. He was nothing like Marvel. And Toya needed to make a decision or lose him for good this time.

"Let me start cleaning this house while my dog is out of the way. I'll see you at Bible study tomorrow."

"Hey, why don't we ride together and then we can go to the mall or something."

Toya thought about the last time she tried to go to the strip mall down the street from Princess's groomer. That episode ended with a panic attack. But Toya wasn't throwing in the towel, maybe she could do it if she went to the mall with Gina. "Sounds like a plan. I'll pick you up in the morning."

14

Today was the final lesson in their Armor of God Bible study. So far, they discovered who the true enemy was and learned that prayer put them right in the presence of God. Then they discussed how the truth of God was core support for the breastplate of righteousness, which was a heavy piece of equipment every soldier must wear. But if the belt of truth were in place, the soldier would be able to stand with righteousness.

Session four was about how the enemy tried to steal our peace of mind, but having our feet shod with the preparation of the gospel of peace would help us withstand those fiery darts the enemy sends our way. And of course, as session five informed them, the shield of faith was one of the most important weapons in spiritual warfare, as the Bible says, 'without faith, it is impossible to please God.'

Toya had always thought that she had faith, but as she listened to Priscilla Shirer describe how faith in God would guide our every action and reaction, she wondered if situations and circumstances had stolen some of her faith. If that was the case, she wanted to get it back. "Increase my faith, Lord," she had prayed during the faith session and the sixth session which had been about salvation.

Finally, today, they were discussing the sword of the spirit, which is the word of God. Priscilla was masterful in the way she

103

taught them that the word of God could be used as a defense mechanism. When the enemy tried to make you believe something about yourself that didn't line up with what God says, put the word on it. The last video was the shortest of all, but as Toya sat listening, she wondered if she had ever truly put the word on her situation. "Help me, Lord."

As the video ended, the lights came back on, and her mother stood behind the pulpit again. "Oh, what a time, what a time," Yvonne Milner-Reed held the microphone to her mouth and yelled through the sanctuary.

"If you leave here the same way you came, you can't blame nobody but yourself. The word was cutting and sharper than a two-edged sword. Oh, taste and see that the Lord is good. He wants His people to truly know Him and understand what His armor can do for them."

Even though no music was playing, women were jumping out of their seats, dancing, shouting, and amening. Yvonne said, "The altar is open, come down here and get what you came for. Ask God to take the fear, shame, and the blame as you put on this armor that God wants you to wear from this day forward.

Just like that, the altar was flooded. Some got on bended knees, some bowed low, and some stood, but all gave praise to God as they called out to Him. Gina had been one of the first women at the altar.

Toya hung back, not wanting the people who had known her most of her life to think that she didn't have all she needed from Jesus. After all, she was the pastor's daughter. But the spirit of God was heavy on her and in the sanctuary. She couldn't deny that she needed something from God.

After Marvel kidnapped her, Toya never said anything to anyone, but she began to doubt God's ability to keep her safe. What was the use in praying, when someone could just snatch you off the street and do what they wanted with you? But as Toya glanced around the room, she came face to face with people, like Mother Thornton, who had been praying for her since she was a child... those prayers, from the people who loved her, was what saved her from a monster like Marvel. Toya needed to get back what she had lost. She had a feeling she would be able to get it right here and right now if she lifted her shield of faith. So, that's what she did. She stood and walked toward the altar; tears streamed down her face as she decided that she wasn't going to leave until she got everything God wanted to give her.

Toya didn't know how she saw it through the blur of tears in her own eyes. But her mother was still standing behind the pulpit, she was no longer instructing the people, she watched Toya's journey to the altar, she got down on the floor and lay prostrate before the Lord. She wasn't saying anything that Toya could make out, she was just crying. But she didn't seem sad, more like tears of joy.

Her mother had been praying for her, and now she finally saw Toya putting her trust in God. Toya felt as if her tears were touching the very hand of Jesus, and He was catching each drop as she poured her heart out to Him. She gave Him her fears and her burdens. When she finally got up and walked back to her seat, Toya truly felt like she could conquer the world. Her fear was gone.

~~~

Later that day Toya and Gina walked the mall and Toya didn't feel the least bit panicked. She had finally learned not just how to use her sword, but how to believe that the word of God was true, and she could trust it. Before leaving church, she wrote in the back of her Bible, 'God has not given me the spirit of fear, but of power, love and of a sound mind.' That scripture came from the book of 2 Timothy 1:7.

Why she hadn't commanded her fear to line up with the word of God before, Toya didn't know, but she would forever be thankful that she attended the Armor of God Bible study.

"How does this look?" Gina had tried on a denim blue jean dress that swayed at the bottom.

"Girl, you are rocking that."

Smiling, while looking in the floor length mirror, Gina said, "I am, aren't I. I'm buying it."

She went back into the dressing room, and Toya picked out a burgundy button-down dress and took it to the dressing room. She had several outfits in burgundy already but loved the color so much, she wasn't opposed to adding another item to her wardrobe.

As she tried on the dress, Toya looked in the mirror and liked what she saw. Not just how the dress looked on her, and it looked amazing. But Toya was enjoying the way her eyes looked because there was no fear, no waiting for the panic attack to begin. Toya gave all glory to God for the way she was feeling. She lifted her hands and praised God inside the dressing room.

Right in the middle of her praise, Toya heard a scream. At first, she wasn't sure it was actually a scream, because she was so caught up in praising the Lord for all He'd done for her. But she quickly received a confirmation with the wrapping on her dressing room door and Gina screaming, "I saw him. I saw him."

Toya opened the dressing room door. "What's going on?" Gina flew inside the dressing room and locked the door behind her. She was shaking so bad; Toya thought her friend was about to have a seizure. Toya put a hand on Gina's shoulder. "Calm down. Tell me what happened."

Gina was crying, "I've been hiding from him for so many years. I thought it was finally safe to come back home. But he found me." Gina was frantic as she added, "He's going to kill me."

"Now that's where you're wrong. Didn't we just finish that Armor of God Bible study? Don't start doubting God's ability to keep you safe. Don't do what I did."

"I just want to get out of here. Can we go now?" Gina was inconsolable.

Toya opened the dressing room door, looked around as if she'd know the guy if she saw him. But since there were only women standing around, she figured it was safe to come out. "I don't see him, Gina. Come on, let's get out of here."

Gina reluctantly stepped out of the dressing room. Everyone in the store was staring at them. "Why are they looking at us?" Gina asked Toya like she hadn't just been screaming her head off.

"Don't worry about them." Toya took the clothes she had worn into the store off the bench and stuffed them in her purse. Thankfully, everyone was too busy staring at them to purchase their items, so the checkout line was empty. Toya quickly purchased the dress, then pulled the tags off of it. She asked the cashier if mall security could escort them to the car.

"I was just about to ask if you needed me to call security," the woman said. She then picked up the phone and did exactly that.

15

Gina was still visibly shaken as Toya drove her home. But she was also embarrassed, so she said, "I'm sorry about all the fuss I made in the store, and how you had to walk out in the dress you were trying on."

"Girl please, I like my dress. I was going to buy it anyway."

"Yeah, but you're weren't planning on wearing it today, were you? It's a really pretty dress, and all we're doing is going home."

Toya put a hand on her friend's shoulder. "Gina, it's alright. I don't know what I would have done if I had seen my ex. And just a few days ago, I had a panic attack when I tried to go to the mall, just thinking about who might be lurking around every corner, so I'm not judging you."

"You've been having panic attacks?"

"I used to have them all the time. That's why I quit my job. But I'm finally free of that."

Gina's eyes narrowed at Toya as her voice raised, "Why didn't you tell me? I've unloaded all of my drama on you and all this time I had no idea that you've been having panic attacks."

Toya could tell that Gina was angry. And she had every right to be because Toya hadn't been totally honest with her friend. She'd sat and listened to Gina tell her whole story of having to move out of the country to get away from some lunatic who didn't know how to say goodbye, and still, she had said nothing of the lunatic that had caused her panic attacks. "I get why you're upset. And you're right. I should have told you what's been going on with me, and I will. Let's go hang out at my place and talk."

Calming down, Gina said, "Thanks, Toya, I really don't think I'm ready to go home by myself."

"What are friends for. You can sleep in the guest room tonight if you want to."

Gina jumped on that. "Let's stop at my place first, so I can get a few things."

They did that, then drove around the corner to Toya's townhouse. Toya made sandwiches and a small side salad for both of them. They sat down in the family room with their food.

Gina said, "I got so worked up, I forgot how hungry I was. She took a few bites of her turkey and swiss sandwich and chewed it like it was lobster. "This is good."

"You must be starving. It's just a turkey sandwich. I wish I had stayed in the kitchen with my mother more and learned how to cook. But I think Tia got that gene. So, I do a bunch of sandwiches around here."

"I understand it. If you look in my kitchen cabinet, you'll see one type of soup after the next. Quick and easy is the way to go when you're just cooking for yourself."

"That's how I see it. But I'm praying that when God sends my husband, the man will know how to cook."

The look on Gina's face changed. Like she was thinking about an unpleasant memory. "You need to be praying for a lot more than that. Trust me, I know."

"You're not alone there," Toya said, as she was now ready to tell her truth. Putting her sandwich down, Toya sighed deeply. "I met this man about a year ago. He was handsome, intelligent, rich, and very attentive. I thought I hit the jackpot. But it turns out that he hated my mother and was only dating me as part of a plot to destroy her."

Gina's head went back as if someone had punched her in the face. "Wait… what did you just say?"

"I know it's hard to believe. But this really happened to me."

"No, it's not hard to believe at all, because I lived with a guy who hated your mother. He blamed her for his mother's death, even though his own father was the one who killed her." Gina rolled her eyes heavenward, then continued, "When I told him that you and I used to be best friends and that your mom was a nice lady, things got crazy between us."

How many men in this world could there possibly be out there hating on her mom? This was no coincidence. "What was his name?"

~~~

Marvel had received word from the private investigator that he had looking for Toya that she was once again attending her mom's church. The investigator said that she had been attending service on Saturdays at eleven in the morning for the last few weeks, so he waited in the parking lot to see which car she would get into. And surprise, surprise.

Not only did Toya walk out of that church, but his long-lost love, Gina was also with her. He had waisted two years of his life searching for that woman. When he finally discovered that she had left the country, he took the hint. She no longer wanted to be with him. He decided to let Gina have fun thinking that she was out of his reach because he needed to focus on putting his plan together so that he could destroy Yvonne Milner.

But now that he had both women in his sight, Marvel figured he must have been living right. Because God was allowing him to kill two birds with one stone. He followed them to the mall and then put a tracking device on Toya's car.

Since he was able to track them to wherever they decided to go next, Marvel didn't have to follow them into the mall. But he couldn't resist letting Gina know that he finally had her in his sights again. She would pay for what she put him through. By the time he was through with Gina, she would beg him to take her back.

His dad told him that in the end, his mom had begged for her life and promised that she would never leave him again. But he just couldn't trust her anymore. Gina had done nothing to make him believe that he could trust her either. And he sure couldn't trust Toya. That one was cut from the same cloth as her mother. She was probably poisoning Gina against him at this very moment.

Women needed to know their place. It is always behind a man, not beside him and certainly not out in front trying to outshine him. He would teach them both a lesson they wouldn't soon forget.

~~~

"Marvel Williams."

Toya fell back in her seat as if a strong wind had swept her away. "This cannot be happening. You and I must truly be attracted to the same kind of men. Because I actually dated that monster."

"Oh, he doesn't come off as a monster at first. He acts more like a Jarrod... kind, attentive, making you feel like he wants to give you the world. But it's all an act." Gina jaw tightened as she spoke of Marvel.

111

Toya shook her head at the memories. "My mom tried to warn me about him, but I wouldn't listen. Marvel seemed to know me so well, my likes, and even the things I didn't like, he didn't like them either. I thought he was the one, so I ignored my mother."

"You can blame me for that," Gina said as sorrow filled her eyes. Then she tried to explain herself. "I was just so terrified of him; I never knew what would set him off and land me in the ER. So, I tried my best to keep him calm."

Toya sympathized with her friend, she recognized the monster in Marvel at the end of their relationship, but Gina lived with him. "Don't be too hard on yourself, Gina. You did what you needed to do in order to survive."

Tears drifted down Gina's face. She hit her thigh with her fist. "He was always in a pleasant and calm mood whenever I told stories about all the fun you and I used to have. I thought he was just being nice to me to make up for slapping or pushing me, or even that time, he blacked my eye and broke my arm.

"But to be truthful, I didn't bother to analyze it too much. Telling my childhood stories kept him calm, and I needed him calm so I could devise a plan of escape." She looked back at Toya, her eyes implored Toya to understand. "But I never thought he would use those stories to hurt you. I promise I would have just let him beat me rather than turn him loose on you."

"I believe you, Gina. You are good with me. And don't worry about Marvel, because we are going to fight this monster together."

Gina's eyes widened with fear. "You don't know him like I do, Toya. The evil that's in him comes from his father. And that man is on a whole nother level of evil. You remember that guy who ran over the woman in Charlottesville or the man who went into that movie theater and shot and killed all those innocent people." Toya nodded. "Well, Marvel Senior is that level of evil."

"You met him?"

Gina shivered as if trying to get a bug off her. "It was about five years ago. Marvel wanted to visit his father. He wanted to introduce me as his future wife to that evil man. Marvel Senior was in a high-security prison, which I totally understood why after our visit. But I had to go through all these security clearances just to have my name added to the list. The first time he hit me was when I said I didn't want to go through all of that just to sit in a prison with someone for thirty minutes.

"He apologized profusely, and I believed that he hadn't meant to do it... until I visited his father. That man took one look at me, then turned to his son as if I wasn't sitting right across from him and said, 'you'll have to beat this one to keep her in line.'"

"No, he didn't." Toya couldn't believe what she was hearing. How could anyone be like that?

"That wasn't all. He had some sort of sick hold over Marvel. He told his son that he wasn't happy with the amount of money that he sent every month. He basically blamed Marvel for his imprisonment. He told Marvel that if his silly mother hadn't got herself knocked up, he wouldn't have married her and therefore, he wouldn't be in this situation. So, it was Marvel's responsibility to take care of him."

"Okay yes, the man is evil," Toya agreed with Gina, but then she said, "But it is our responsibility to put the word of God on this situation. Don't let Marvel make you forget what we learn in Bible study. You're fearful because of all that you know about Marvel, right?"

Gina's hands were folded in her lap as she nodded.

"But the word of God tells us that 'God has not given us the spirit of fear but of love, power land of a sound mind.'"

"I know all of that, Toya, but somehow when it comes to this situation with Marvel, I forget about God and start worrying about what Marvel is going to do next."

"That's fair, because like you said, you are afraid."

"Aren't you afraid too?"

"I'm not superhuman, so I do have some fear for the situation, especially because Marvel kidnapped me at gunpoint and had plans to kill me."

Snapping her fingers, Gina said, "That's why you started having panic attacks, isn't it?"

"At first, I was okay. People had prayed for me and then I was rescued from Marvel. But later when I had time by myself, I allowed thoughts to flood in... like, why did anyone have to pray about that situation at all? Couldn't God have stopped Marvel from kidnapping me if he had wanted to? Then I thought about my father's untimely death and that's when the panic attacks began because I just didn't trust God anymore.

"I never wanted to admit that to anyone, because how do you tell your pastor parents that you don't trust God? I'm just so thankful that you called and asked me to attend that Bible study. Each week, my faith kept growing, and I realized that although things do happen in this world that God still loves me. And if He won't give up on me, I sure won't ever give up on Him again, no matter what."

"I wish I was more like you."

Toya shook her head. "You don't have to be like me. Just remember God's word. Take the scripture we just talked about... if God hasn't given us the spirit of fear, then what has He given us."

Gina answered, "Power, love and a sound mind."

"Exactly. But let's not just say the words without dissecting it. Now when I hear the word power, it tells me that I have the power to trust God. I have the power to do something about the situation I'm in, like call the police and alert them to the fact that Marvel Williams is back in town." As Toya picked up her phone to call the police, she asked Gina, "What does the word power make you think of?"

"I guess," she began a little timid at first, "I have the power to pray rather than worry about things I can't control in the first place."

Toya high five'd her. "And it's prayer that helps us to have that sound mind that God wants to give us." After saying that, Toya called the police and informed them that the man she has a protective order against was now back in town.

When she hung up with the police, she called her mother and warned her that Marvel was in town, "Be careful Mom, okay."

"I will, hon. But I'm more concerned about you. Maybe Thomas and I should drive over there and bring you to the house with us."

"I'm good Mom. Gina and I are hanging out. She's going to spend the night with me." She didn't bother to tell her mom that Gina was staying over because she was the one who was terrified of Marvel. If Gina wanted anyone else to know her business, she would have to tell them.

When Toya hung up, Gina said, "About that prayer. Do you think we can do some of that now?"

"Absolutely."

16

"Oh no she's not staying at her place tonight. I'll go get her myself and bring her back here," Jarrod said as his father informed him that Marvel was back in town. "That man won't lay a finger on her as long as I'm still living."

"Calm down, Son. Toya has already called the police and she lives in a secure community."

"I know all that, Dad. But I also know how terrified she has been these last few months. That man stole her peace of mind. She's just now starting to come back to herself, and there is no way I'm going to just sit back and watch her fall apart again." Jarrod took his keys off the counter and headed for the backyard. Princess had gotten so big that Yvonne wouldn't allow her in the house. "Thanks for inviting me to dinner, but I've got to go."

Yvonne and Thomas looked at each other, their eyes communicating something that the two of them now understood clearly. Thomas walked out the front door and waited while Jarrod put the dog in the back seat of the car. The dogs head was touching the roof of the car. "You're going to need something bigger to transport Princess in."

"Yeah, I know. Her growth exploded in the last month." Jarrod got behind the wheel of the car.

Thomas stepped back, but before his son pulled off, he said, "You really love her, don't you?"

"That's what I've been trying to tell you," Jarrod shook his head in frustration. No matter how old they got, their parents still saw them as teenagers and wouldn't understand that the mistakes of the past had nothing to do with what was going on now.

"I get it, Son. I get it. Just remember, these Milner women might be stubborn, but they have good hearts. Don't let her get away this time."

Backing out of the driveway, Jarrod said, "I won't. And I won't let Marvel get to her either as God is my witness."

"We'll be praying for you." Thomas went back in the house and he and Yvonne touched and agreed on the safety of both their children as they prayed.

~~~

Marvel pulled up to the guard shack with a Pizza Hut hat on and the pizza warmer bag in the back seat. When the guard greeted him, Marvel rolled down his window and said, "I have a pizza delivery for 1922 Ferguson Street."

"Wrong block. There's no Ferguson in this community." He shewed him away with the back of his hand. "Back up and turn around."

"Yo-Yo, my man. I think I just got the street name wrong. My boss told me that the pizza has to be delivered to Moss Creek, this is the Moss, right?"

"Yeah, this is the Moss, but our residents call down to inform me whenever they order out. And I don't have Pizza Hut on my call list."

"Let me check my delivery list." Marvel looked around in the front seat, then jabbed his forehead with his index finger. "I can't believe I did that. I put the delivery list in my trunk." He opened the door, and before the guard could say anything, he popped the trunk. "Let me show you the address, then you can tell me where to go."

"Get back in your car," the guard yelled at him.

"Come on, man, I'm going to lose my job if I don't deliver these pizzas." Instead of getting a delivery list out of his trunk, he lifted a sawed-off shotgun, cocked it and then pointed it at the guard's head. "Open the gate."

The guard's hands went up. "Man, what's going on? I know you don't need to deliver pizzas this bad."

Marvel walked over to the guard and asked, "Do you want to live or die tonight?"

"I got kids, man. I want to live."

"Open the gate. And I guarantee you, I won't ask again."

The guard hit a button, and the gate slide open. Marvel then whacked the guard in the head with the shotgun. He then shoved the guard in the back of his car and pulled the rope out of his pizza warmer bag and tied the guy up.

Marvel got back in the car and drove into one of the safest communities in Detroit like he owned the place and was riding through to check on the upkeep of his property.

~~~

Toya and Gina had changed into their pajamas and were lounging in the family room watching a movie and chilling out.

Gina took a deep breath. "I think I have actually calmed down. Thanks for helping me to see things differently today."

"What are friends for."

"Hey, remember when had that pajama party at your house and the boys stood outside the house throwing rocks at your bedroom window?"

Toya laughed. "It was Jarrod and his goofy friends. I remember one of them had a serious crush on you, so Jarrod was trying to play matchmaker."

"Sureeee, if you say so… he was trying to play matchmaker. But I think he was just itching for another chance to be close to you."

"He had a funny way of showing it if that was his plan." Toya rolled her eyes at the thought.

"That's why he beat up that guy who started gyrating and made a few off-color remarks about what you could do for him."

Snapping her finger, Toya said, "I remember that. It was Hank Gilbert, and do you know that pervert actually became a preacher."

"Jesus probably got a hold of him right after Jarrod put that beat down on him," Gina and Toya laughed.

But then Toya said, "Actually it was my dad. Remember he chased the guys off, but I wondered how come it took him an extra few minutes to get outside with all the noise the fight was causing. Turns out, Dad heard what Hank said to me, and he let Jarrod get in a few punches before breaking it up. But later, Dad told me that he felt bad that he hadn't prayed for Hank. So, that's what he started doing, and then he eventually became his mentor."

"Your dad was an awesome man," Gina told her.

"Yes, he was." Toya smiled at the memories. "From that day forward, Jarrod could do no wrong in his eyes. Whenever Jarrod would come for a visit, Dad would always tell me, 'that boy is going to be something in this world.'"

"You think he was trying to send you subliminal messages about Jarrod?"

"If that's what he was doing, I wish he would have come right out and said, 'this is the guy for you' because I just don't know what to do with that man."

119

"Well, you better figure it out, because he is coming for you. I'm just proud of him for finally opening up and telling you how he feels."

Toya thought about that for a moment. "I wish he had done it sooner; things are just too complicated now."

"Girl, love is love, and ain't nothing complicated about that."

"Actually, some love is just lust and should never ever happen in the first place."

"Do you think that Jarrod is only feeling lust for you?"

Toya shook her head. "We've known each other too long for that. Look, just ignore me. I'm too confused right now to know what to do about anything."

Gina turned off the television and stood. "I'm drained. It's bedtime for me."

"Sounds like a plan. If we're going to make the first service at church tomorrow, I think we'd better get some sleep."

~~~

The tracker Marvel put on Toya's car had malfunctioned, it directed him to Toya's subdivision with no problem. But once he drove through the gates, the signal went haywire, causing him to drive around in circles. Marvel pulled over to the side of the street, reached in the back and shook the guard until he woke up.

The man was stretched out in the back of the car with his arms and feet tied yet Marvel still put the barrel of the gun in his face. "Where does Toya Milner live?"

"Who?"

"Don't play games with me, not if you want to make it home to see them kids of yours."

120

The guard huffed. "Do you think I'm dumb enough to believe that you're going to let me live." The guard spit at him. "Find her yourself."

Marvel would have loved nothing more than to put a bullet in this man's head. But the sound of the shotgun would alert the neighbors, and he still remembered how a noisy neighbor had stopped him from finishing off Toya the last time. So, he put the gun down and punched him so hard it knocked him out.

Marvel woke him up again. "How many times do you think that pee brain of yours can take being knocked out?" Marvel lifted his fist again.

"Wait… wait… wait."

But Marvel hit him anyway, then asked, "What's the address?"

His nose was bleeding, and his jaw was beginning to swell. "Toya is a nice lady. Why do you want to bother her?"

"Last chance." Marvel pulled a pair of bolt cutters out of the glove compartment and started towards the guard with them.

"Around the corner, man. She leaves on the next street over." The guard cried as he gave up the information. He really liked Toya and hated that this man would be anywhere near her.

17

"Did you hear something." Gina came barreling out of the guest bedroom and banging on Toya's bedroom door.

Toya yawned and stretched as she got out of bed. She unlocked her bedroom door, and as she opened it, Gina flew in. "I thought you were sleep. What woke you?"

"I heard something."

Yawning again, Toya said, "I fell asleep the minute my head hit the pillow. I didn't hear anything." But as soon as she said that, there was a loud crash, like a window breaking in the kitchen. "Oh, my God." Toya turned to Gina. "Call the police."

She then went into her closet and grabbed the big stick she kept tucked away in there. Toya never liked the idea of keeping a gun in the house for protection... too many things could go wrong. But this stick would help her wail on an intruder.

But when she reached the living room on her way to the kitchen to see why glass was breaking, Gina was standing in the entry between both rooms staring at something that caused her to freeze with the phone in her hand. "Did you call the police?" Toya asked as she turned to look at what Gina was staring at. Marvel was coming through the window.

Toya ran towards him with her stick as she said, "Call the police now!"

As if coming out of a trance, Gina dialed 911. Toya gave a good swing and knocked Marvel back out of the window. "And stay out," she yelled at him.

"Help, we have an intruder," Gina said as an operator came on the line. She was in the process of giving them Toya's address as Marvel banged against the back door so hard that the door jamb broke.

"Get out of here, Gina."

"I can't leave you with that monster," Gina protested.

"You have too. Go get us some help."

Gina nodded. "Okay, right," she ran towards the front door.

Marvel burst through the back door and yelled at Gina as she tried to flee. "You get back here. You're not going anywhere until I say so."

"She doesn't answer to you anymore. You don't scare us." He laughed at that but stopped laughing when Toya swung that stick and caught him in the chest. She heard the cracking of his ribs as he went down. Toya felt like a champion with the armor of God on. She looked to heaven and silently said, 'this battle is not mine alone, Lord. It's yours, so give me the strength to fight.'

"You've got some arm there, but I've got something better," he told her.

Toya was about to swing on him again, but he pulled a gun from his back pocket. "You're evil," she spat the words at him.

"How is your mother?" He was holding his rib cage with one hand and had the gun pointed at her with his other hand.

"My mother is none of your concern. You need help, Marvel. You had everything a man could want with Gina. But you destroyed

123

that relationship and almost destroyed her all because you can't stop hating."

"Yes, I hate. I hate the fact that you have a mother, but mine is dead. Why should your mother live in peace after destroying my family?"

"Your father destroyed your family, and if you weren't so mental, you'd be able to see that."

"Shut-up and get over here, or I'll shoot you where you stand."

~~~

"Is that You, Lord?" This was Mother Thornton's normal question whenever she awoke out of her sleep and still felt restless even after using the bathroom.

The Lord had her on prayer assignments. She never knew who or what she would be required to pray for on any given night, she was just thankful that the Lord trusted her with the assignment. Mother Thornton was up in age, almost ninety, so her knees didn't tolerate bending like they used to.

She couldn't bend down on the floor and pray, but she had a special prayer chair in her bedroom. Mother Thornton got out of bed and sat in her chair and began praying in her heavenly language. A few minutes after she started praying in tongues, Mother Thornton saw the face of Toya and Gina pass before her. At first, she thought she only saw their faces because she had just been at Bible study with them.

But then she reminded herself that there were no coincidences in the spirit realm. The Lord Jesus wanted her to pray for those two sweet young ladies and she would do just that, even if she had to stay up all night long. "Deliver them, Jesus."

~~~

As Jarrod drove over to Toya's place, he chided himself for being a lovesick puppy. Toya was safe. She lived in a great community with a guard and a locked gate. You couldn't just bust into the Moss.

"You think Toya's going to be mad at us for coming back a day early?" Jarrod asked Princess.

Princess had been in the back seat minding her own business, but when Jarrod spoke to her, she jumped from the back to the front and barked.

"You want to hang out with me for another night? You think we should just go home and see Toya in the morning?"

Princess barked again, but this time she shook her head.

"Ain't that about nothing. Well, I have more fun with Toya too. But she did ask for a break." But hey, if Princess was homesick and wanted to be with Toya, what could he do but comply with the dog.

Jarrod kept driving toward Toya's place. When he got there and saw the gate wide open, and the guard missing in action. He was immediately fearful that something had happened to Toya. As he drove through the gates, he called his dad and said, "Something's wrong, Dad. I need you to pray like only you know how."

"I'm going to pray, Son. But it's time for you to do the same. Remember what I told you."

Hanging up the phone, Jarrod was so worried that Toya was in danger that he couldn't do anything else but pray as he kept driving towards her townhouse. "We need You, God. We need You to come through for us. Protect Toya. Don't let harm come to her, Lord. Yes, I'm talking to You Lord... my Lord. The One I have trusted all these years, and I want to trust You with this situation too. Please come through for us." Tears bubbled in Jarrod's eyes, causing him to not be able to see clearly. But he kept driving anyway.

"No Father, I'm not begging You as if you are some stranger and I'm not sure how great You are, or all the marvelous things You have done. So, right now I'm just going to thank You for helping us. Toya will survive this night, and she will not withdraw and hide away ever again, in Jesus name. I count it done, Amen."

For the first time in Jarrod's life, he felt a tug in his spirit, like God was listening to him and was working things out. He'd never felt like that before. No prayer, he'd ever prayed had mattered to him as much as this one. Life was breaking him down and causing him to see just how much he needed God... he couldn't do this by himself.

Princess barked and barked. Then she reached around him and blew the horn several times. Jarrod stopped the car and wiped the tears from his eyes. That's when he saw Gina running in the street, screaming for help at the top of her lungs.

He blew the horn for her, rolled down his window and waved at her. "Gina, it's me, Jarrod."

Gina ran over to the car. "Thank God, it's you. Marvel has Toya in the house. She held him off so I could run to get help." Gina jumped in the car with him, and they turned the corner.

As they pulled up to the side of Toya's townhouse, Jarrod noticed the car that was parked in-between Toya's place and her neighbors. The headlights were off, but the car was still running. "Have you seen this car before. Do the neighbors have company?"

"I don't know. I wasn't paying attention. I just started running."

Jarrod got out of the car and slowly walked over to the other car. A shotgun was in the front seat, and a man was tied up in the back seat of the car. The man in the back seat, shook his head as if he was just waking up. Jarrod recognized him.

He tried the door, and it opened. The first thing Jarrod did was take the key out of the ignition and put it in his pocket. He then untied the security guard. The man looked like he'd been worked over pretty good.

"Did he hurt her?" The guard asked as he rubbed his arms and legs.

"I hope not. I'm going in the house now."

"We're going to need this." The guard took the shotgun off the front seat. "That man has a hard-right hook."

~~~

"What's that?" Marvel said as he grabbed hold of Toya's arm, getting ready to escort her to his car. But a horn was honking, just like last time. "If that old lady is out there beating on my car again, I'm going to shoot her this time."

"What old lady? What are you talking about?" Marvel might have a gun on her, but Toya wasn't afraid of him this time. Instead, she chose to believe God. He could protect her, and if this didn't end the way she wanted it to, she would be in heaven, so she wins either way.

"Don't you worry about it. Just know that I've got it handled." He glanced out the window and saw that the guard was being untied. He then saw the guard grab his shotgun. "Why did I leave that," he mumbled to himself. Then he put a tighter hold on Toya. "Come on."

"No, let me go."

"You are going with me. I'm not letting you get away from me this time." Marvel tried to grip Toya's arm tighter. But he couldn't hold both arms since he had the gun in his other hand.

Toya decided that she wasn't going to let Marvel trample all over her without a fight. She swung on him, connecting her fist with his jaw. It caught him off guard, so he wobbled backward and dropped the gun. Toya dived on the floor towards the gun.

"Oh no you don't." Marvel pulled her back as he got down on the floor with her. They tussled. Toya drug her sharp fingernails across Marvel's pretty boy face. Marvel yelled and then snatched a handful of Toya's hair as he smacked her.

Toya's wasn't fazed, she wanted to fight back. She had the Armor of God on her side and she wasn't going down like some punk who didn't know the power they possessed. But Marvel got hold of the gun and put it to her head. "Get up and walked out this door with me, or I will leave your brains splattered all over this floor for your mother to see."

Toya couldn't imagine what seeing something like that could do to a mother. She just knew that she couldn't let it end here, so she did as Marvel instructed. As she stood, he took the electrical tape off one of the loops on his pants. He put a piece across Toya's mouth and then pulled her out the back door. "What? Whatcha say I can't understand you." He mocked her as she tried to scream with the tape on her mouth. He roughly guided her through the back yard and into the woods out back.

Toya's words could not be heard by the human ear because of the tape on her mouth. But God was hearing every word she uttered as she said, "I trust You, Lord. I know that I will soon see the salvation of the Lord. You will save me from this monster. And I thank You. Come see about me, Jesus!" She was bound and determined to keep her armor on, right now she was holding up her shield of faith, letting the Lord know that she would never doubt Him again, no matter the situation or the circumstance. "Fix it, Jesus!"

18

"The house is empty," Jarrod said as he and the guard stamped through it.

"He must've taken her into the woods. There's no light back there so we'll have to wait for the police before we can do anything."

"I'm not waiting for nobody." Jarrod went back to the car and got Princess. He took her to Toya's room and picked up one of her shirts that were on the floor in her closet. Princess sniffed the shirt, then barked. "Let's go find her, girl." Jarrod took a flashlight out of the kitchen drawer, then walked with Princess into the woods. The guard followed behind him with the shotgun.

"Is she out here, girl?"

Princess barked and then barked again. She kept barking and wiggling as if she wanted to be free. Jarrod took her off the lease. "Go get her, Princess. Bring Toya back to us."

Princess took off so fast that Jarrod and the guard had to run at top speed just to keep her in their sights. "Get her, girl," Jarrod yelled as Princess bark changed to a howling sound.

"Stay back. Don't you come any closer."

Jarrod heard the man yell at Princess and then he heard the shot as Princess pounced on the man. "No!" Jarrod screamed.

Princess had jumped on top of Marvel, but the dog had been wounded. She whimpered as blood oozed from her belly.

The guard cocked the gun as Marvel tried to stand. "You're done. Make another move, and I'll end it all for you right now."

Marvel threw the gun about five feet away from him as the guard lifted him off the ground and walked him out of the woods.

Jarrod pulled the tape from Toya's mouth as they both clung to Princess.

"No, no, no." Toya was beside herself with grief as Princess laid there whimpering from the pain she felt. She rubbed the dog.

Jarrod put the electrical tape that had been over Toya's mouth on the dog's wound. He then took his jacket off and tied it around the dog to slow the bleeding. "I'm going to need your help," he told Toya.

Toya was beside herself with grief. She clung to Princess as if holding her tight would keep her with them forever.

"Toya, come on. I need your help."

The tears were flowing so fast that she could barely speak. "Wh.. what are... are we going to do?"

"We've got to carry her out of the woods, or she won't get any help. I'll pick her up from the bottom, and you'll have to get her head."

"I can do that," Toya said through her tears. She kissed Princess's fur. "Thank you, Princess. But now we need to help you." They picked her up. Princess moaned and looked at Toya with sad eyes. Toya couldn't stop crying. She loved her dog. "Please, God, let her be alright."

Once they were out of the woods, Gina ran over to them. Jarrod told them, "Stay right here so I can get the car and drive her to the vet."

"The police are here. They just took Marvel," Gina told Toya as they both crouched down around Princess.

The two women hugged. "I told you we had nothing to fear."

"I'm so sorry about Princess. Do you think she'll be okay?" Gina asked.

"If she lives long enough for us to get her to the vet, she might have a fighting chance." Toya rubbed Princess and put her mouth close to the dog's ear. "You're going to be okay, Princess. You are my brave, brave dog, and you are going to be with Jarrod and me for a very long time. Stay with us, Princess. Don't leave me now, okay. I promise I'll take you for as many walks as you want and I won't complain."

Jarrod pulled up, and they took the dog to the only vet they could find that was still open. Thankfully, this vet was able to perform surgery on Princess immediately. Now, they were just sitting in the waiting room with their family as they waited to find out whether Princess would survive Marvel's cruelty.

"I'm just so thankful that you are alright," Yvonne said as she hugged Toya. "I don't know what I would have done if that man had hurt you."

"No one will be hurt by Marvel again for a long time. He is going to sit in prison and rot. And for that I'm thankful," Gina said with that wonderful spark in her eyes that had dwindled the moment she saw Marvel in the mall.

Toya held onto her friend's hand. "No one will ever hurt you again, Gina. We found the secret, remember."

Gina nodded, "The Armor of God will protect us from now and evermore."

"That's right," Yvonne agreed, so happy that Toya and Gina truly took hold of the message of the study.

"Wow," Thomas said, "If that Bible study stuck like that for the women, maybe we should do something for the men. What do you say, Jarrod? You want to help your old man put a men's program together?"

Head bobbing, Jarrod said, "I could do that."

The vet came into the waiting room, the look on his face didn't give away anything. Jarrod took Toya by the hand and helped her stand up. They would face whatever was to come together. "Tell us straight, Doc. How is she?"

"She's resting. It was a good thing that the bullet missed all her internal organs. It entered and exited without damaging anything. So, all I had to do was sew her back up to stop the bleeding."

"Praise God." Toya was so happy, she let Jarrod pull her into an embrace even while her family watched.

He kissed her, as he pulled back, he said, "I love you, Toya, always have."

She stood there looking at him for what seemed like forever. At first, she wasn't sure how to respond. This was all new to her, but Jarrod had come to her rescue again as he always had and always would. "Ditto, Bubba. I love you too."

Jarrod shook his head. "I don't know who Bubba is, but you better get him off your mind and focus on me, because I will fight him if I have to."

"You won't have to fight, I promise, I will leave Bubba alone for good."

"And so, it begins for us." Toya and Jarrod had a lot to work out, but they were on the same page now. Not only that, they had God on their side, and a threefold cord is not easily broken.

Epilogue

"Mom, are you in here?" Toya asked as she walked into the fellowship hall. Her mother had asked that she meet up with her at the church, but when she arrived all the lights were off. Toya thought that was strange, but she tried the door to the fellowship hall anyway. It opened.

When she stepped in, the lights came on, but they were dim. Glancing around the room, she saw huge balloons floating around the ceiling. The balloons had light strings that clung to them while the remaining string hung in the air creating a spectacular display.

There was a table off to the left that had punch, cake, and finger sandwiches on it. A backdrop clung to the back wall of the fellowship hall with black and blue letters that said Prom 2005. "What is going on here?"

Jarrod walked into the room wearing a black tuxedo with a baby blue shirt. He was holding out a corsage to her. "I figured since people do throwback parties all the time, why couldn't we do a throwback of our own."

"You are actually trying to recreate our prom." She looked so confused as she glanced around the room again. "But how? Why? I don't have anything to wear."

He pointed toward the bookstore. "Everything you need is waiting behind that door." He turned her in the direction of the bookstore and nudged her forward.

Looking back at Jarrod, she said, "But you didn't have to do this. I mean, we are thirty-two years old. What business do we have at a prom?"

"Woman, just do what I tell you, for once in your life."

Toya opened the door and stepped into the bookstore. Her mother and Gina were inside waiting for her. "Both of you knew about this, and you didn't say anything to me?"

Grinning from ear to ear, Yvonne said, "Didn't Jarrod just tell you to hush that fuss?"

"Mom you don't care about this kind of stuff. You weren't even home to help me get dressed for actually senior prom."

"I'm here now," Yvonne told her. "And I'm going to enjoy every moment of this prom with you."

"But Mom, I just don't get why he's doing this. And why you allowed him to decorate the fellowship hall like that."

Gina interrupted her friend. "Have a seat, my lady. The ball is about to begin, and we need to do your hair and make-up."

"You're serious. We are really doing this?"

Her mother nodded, then pointed toward the chair.

Toya sat down. On the table next to the chair was a curling iron, hair products and all sorts of make-up. "Where did you get all of this stuff from?"

"After my dad got laid off from his job, I had to model the last two years of college to pay my way."

"That sounds exciting," Toya said, seeing another side of her friend.

"Believe me, it wasn't. But at least I have my degree. The make-up is a side bonus. I've probably thrown away half of all the goop I acquired during those days."

"Okay, so you're going to take care of my hair and make-up. But Jarrod is standing out there in a whole tuxedo."

Yvonne walked over to one of the racks in the bookstore and came back carrying this amazing baby blue strapless dress with a sequin halter. Below the halter was a silky long flowing skirt. Toya would have picked this dress out herself if she had seen it. "It's beautiful, Mom. Thank you."

"Don't thank me. Jarrod picked this dress out. He knows you just as much as I do. I finally realized that when I saw the dress. I actually pictured you in this thing. And now you're about to put it on and go to your prom."

Toya hopped out of her seat and hugged her mother. She then said, "Okay, let's do this."

Within thirty minutes, Toya was dressed, her hair was in an updo, and her make-up was fresh. As she walked back into the fellowship hall, which was now the location of her prom, music began to play. Jarrod was standing in the middle of the floor, holding a handout for her. "Can I have this dance?"

"Well Bubba, since you went to all this trouble, how can I not dance with you?" Toya took his hand and allowed Jarrod to pull her into his arms. They swayed to the music and Toya had to admit that being in Jarrod's arms felt good. Oh, so good.

"Why did you do all of this?" She asked as they gazed into each other's eyes.

"For your love, baby, I would do anything. Even go back to 2005, one of the worst years of my life."

Her eyes questioned him. "What made 2005 so bad. We graduated high school and set off for college. We were becoming, developing, and growing back then."

"All of that was cool. But 2005 was the year I had to say goodbye to you. All else paled compared to the pain I endured.

"Ah, baby." She ran her hands over his head and kissed him like he was the very air she breathed, and without him, she wouldn't survive.

They danced, ate snacks, and drank punch. Thomas even entered the room and played photographer for them. By the time she and Jarrod stood in front of their prom backdrop, she was completely convinced that this prom was better than anything she would have ever experience back in high school. Because now she was convinced that what she and Jarrod had was real.

Things got real, real when Jarrod dropped down on one knee in front of their parents and her best friend and said, "Toya, I have loved you for so long that I can't remember a time when I wasn't in love with you. I need you in my life. Will you please marry me?"

Yep, this was the best prom ever. "Yes!" She shouted and then Jarrod took her in his arms and swung her around. They were always meant to be together. Time, distance and other opportunities… nothing was strong enough to keep them apart and nothing from this day forward would ever come between them again.

The end… of this one, but the saga continues in Book 3

(Got To Be Love) Coming in September 2019… Got To Be Love
(Book 3 in the Loving You Series)

Don't forget to join my mailing list:
http://vanessamiller.com/events-join-mailing-list/
Join me on Facebook: https://www.facebook.com/groups/
77899021863/
Join me on Twitter: https://www.twitter.com/
vanessamiller01

Books in the Loving You Series

Our Love

For Your Love

Got To Be Love

Releases September 2019

Other Books by Vanessa Miller

Family Business I
Family Business II
Family Business III
Family Business IV
Family Business V

Family Business VI

Our Love

For Your Love

Got To Be Love

Rain in the Promised Land

Heaven Sent

Sunshine And Rain

After the Rain

How Sweet The Sound

Heirs of Rebellion

Feels Like Heaven

Heaven on Earth

The Best of All

Better for Us

Her Good Thing

Long Time Coming

A Promise of Forever Love

A Love for Tomorrow

Yesterday's Promise

Forgotten

Forgiven

Forsaken

Rain for Christmas (Novella)

Through the Storm

Rain Storm

Latter Rain

Abundant Rain

Former Rain

Anthologies (Editor)

Keeping the Faith

Have A Little Faith

This Far by Faith

Novella

Love Isn't Enough

A Mighty Love

The Blessed One (Blessed and Highly Favored series)

The Wild One (Blessed and Highly Favored Series)

The Preacher's Choice (Blessed and Highly Favored Series)

The Politician's Wife (Blessed and Highly Favored Series)

The Playboy's Redemption (Blessed and Highly Favored Series)

Tears Fall at Night (Praise Him Anyhow Series)

Joy Comes in the Morning (Praise Him Anyhow Series)

A Forever Kind of Love (Praise Him Anyhow Series)

Ramsey's Praise (Praise Him Anyhow Series)

Escape to Love (Praise Him Anyhow Series)

Praise For Christmas (Praise Him Anyhow Series)

His Love Walk (Praise Him Anyhow Series)

Could This Be Love (Praise Him Anyhow Series)

Song of Praise (Praise Him Anyhow Series)

Sample read...

Our Love

Book 1

Loving You Series

By

Vanessa Miller

Prologue

On days like this, Yvonne Milner wondered why she even bothered to pray. She had yelled, screamed, begged, and cajoled, yet the doctors still couldn't make eye contact with her when they came into her husband's hospital room. There were no more talks of surgery or chemotherapy. They'd told her that nothing more could be done for David. But, as far as Yvonne was concerned, the doctors didn't know diddly. David Milner was the senior pastor of one of the most notable churches in Detroit. He was the father of two beautiful daughters, and he was her beloved husband. So, she wasn't just going to throw in the towel and believe the doctors' doom-and-gloom predictions. She and David had been married for thirty-four years, and he had promised her a fiftieth wedding anniversary celebration. "We've got sixteen more years to go, David," she urged him. "Don't give up now."

A vicious cough shook his fragile, cancer-racked body as he attempted to sit up in his hospital bed.

"Don't, sweetheart. Just lie down."

"No…I need…to tell you…something." David labored to get each word out.

It was killing Yvonne to see her husband weak and bedridden like this. He had always been so strong, had always been her hero. She had admired this man, even when they hadn't seen eye-to-eye about her role in the ministry. Early in their marriage, Yvonne had known that she was destined to preach the gospel. However, David wouldn't hear of it. They had fought, and Yvonne had prayed for years that God would change her husband's mind. Finally, David had accepted the fact that his wife had been called by God to be a preacher. Yet, even through those tough years, Yvonne couldn't have imagined being anywhere else but with the man she loved. "You can say what you need to while lying down, honey. You need your strength to get better."

David shook his head. "I'm going home, baby."

"I know that, David. You just need to regain your strength so they will let you out of this hospital."

He shook his head again and then pointed heavenward. "Home… with Jesus."

Yvonne's eyes filled with tears. "Don't say that, David. You and I have a lot more living to do."

He patted her hand. "Call Thomas."

Thomas Reed was David's best friend. The man traveled the world building churches and ministering to God's people. He'd recently lost his wife to the same evil disease that was threatening to take David's life. "Call Thomas right now? Why? What do you want me to tell him?"

"If you need help, call Thomas. He promised me—" A coughing fit cut him off.

Yvonne took the cup from David's bedside table and filled it with water from the pitcher, then held the glass to his lips for him to drink once the coughing subsided. "Here, baby, drink this." When he had taken a few sips, she said, "Now, just lie here and rest. Our girls will be here soon, and you need to save your energy for them." Toya, twenty-nine years old, was their firstborn, a self-assured attorney with political aspirations. Tia was their twenty-six-year-old "baby." Whereas Toya was analytical and ambitious, Tia's strength was creativity, yet she was introspective and reserved. She could paint and write poetry from sunup till sundown and be perfectly at peace.

It had been difficult for Yvonne to manage her daughters' very different personalities while raising them, but David had convinced her to relax and let God work out His perfect plan for each girl's life. If it hadn't been for David's wisdom and prayers, Yvonne was sure that she would have broken Tia's spirit. She had needed more time than David to understand their daughter's passion for writing and painting. What was she going to do if he didn't survive this illness?

No sooner had the thought crossed her mind than Yvonne tried to banish it. But that was also the moment when she noticed that David's breathing sounded funny. And then she understood why none of the medical professionals who had come into the room today had been able to look her in the eye. They had heard it, too—the death rattle.

"No, baby, no—don't leave me!" she begged him.

"Remember…Thomas promised…love you."

Tears were running down Yvonne's face as she heard her husband's last words. She put her arms around the man she had loved for a lifetime—and yet not long enough—and whispered, "I love you, too, baby. Always and forever."

One

Yvonne Milner collapsed into her office chair and heaved a sigh. Pastoring Christ-Life Sanctuary by herself was far from easy, and it seemed that her situation was only getting worse. For years, the church had grown and thrived, even reaching megachurch status with more than five thousand members. But since David's death, two thousand of their "You can count on me" members had left the ministry. The head elder, Ron Thompson, had broken away to start his own ministry, taking another two hundred church members with him. Tithing was down, charity fund expenditures were up, and Yvonne knew that the church's board of directors blamed it all on her.

Several of the board members had challenged her authority to her face and as good as said that they wouldn't be having those problems if David were still around or if their senior pastor wasn't a woman. Yvonne acknowledged that some people could not accept having a female in the highest position of church leadership, but she also knew that not all twenty-two hundred members had left for that reason.

Sighing again, she stood up and stepped over to the bay window to gaze out at the new Family Life Center—or, rather, what was supposed to be the new Family Life Center, the final phase of their latest building project. The Family Life Center had been Yvonne's vision. After the sanctuary had been expanded to make room for

144

their growing congregation, Yvonne had convinced David that they still needed to do more. She envisioned a brand-new facility that would provide space for recreational activities, especially for the children and young adults, as well as a café and a bookstore. In addition, she intended for one of the rooms to be set up theater-style, with tiered seats and a movie screen, where they could organize movie nights or perform stage plays.

Five years ago, when Yvonne and David had first proposed the building project to the board, they had developed a financial plan based on the church's finances and projected that they would have more than enough funds to cover each phase of the project. But Yvonne hadn't foreseen the death of her husband or the annihilation of Detroit's economy. How could she have known that General Motors and Chrysler would go crying to the government for a bail-out and then lay off thousands upon thousands of workers, many of whom attended church at Christ-Life Sanctuary?

Now Yvonne was stuck staring at a half finished Family Life Center, as it would probably remain. After all, the coffers were empty. She really couldn't blame the board of directors for asking for her resignation. When her husband was alive, Yvonne stood side by side with him as they built this church from the ground up. She had installed three of their seven board members herself. And she knew that God wasn't finished with her yet. The work He had begun in her—and in the church through her ministry—was far from over, and she would be dead and buried before anyone took her out of the pulpit permanently. She just needed a plan, needed to pray about knowing the right things to say at the board meeting tomorrow in order to convince the members to give her more time to turn things around.

A knock at her door drew Yvonne's eyes away from the window. She turned toward the door. "Come in."

The door opened, and in walked Thomas Reed. Actually, he didn't walk; he swaggered like a man who had the keys to the kingdom. If she hadn't known Thomas for almost thirty years, Yvonne would have thought he swaggered so confidently because he was a millionaire several times over. But Thomas had strutted like that even when he had been as poor as a man carrying a "Will work for food" sign.

Thomas had a way about him that caused men and women to stop and stare. He was one of those fine, chocolate, Denzel-Washington-type of brothers, with wavy black hair and heavenly hazel eyes.

David had met Thomas thirty years ago in seminary and had joked about marrying Yvonne to keep her away from pretty boys like Thomas. But David never had reason to worry; he had always been her prince, and she'd never wanted anyone but him.

When Thomas got married, David became less worried about his friend's captivating charm. The four of them—David and Yvonne, Thomas and Brenda—had settled into their own ministries, yet maintained a lasting friendship. David and Yvonne opened Christ-Life Sanctuary a year after David graduated from seminary, and the church had thrived from its inception. Thomas, on the other hand, was forced to close the doors to his church after struggling for five years to make a go of it. He hadn't let that stop him, though. Thomas became a Christ-centered motivational speaker and took his ministry on the road. He now pulled in fifty thousand dollars per speaking engagement and had written nearly a dozen *New York Times* best-selling books.

"Thomas!" Yvonne gave him a hug and stepped back to admire his suit. "Look at you, dapper as ever on this hot summer day."

"You don't look so bad, yourself," he said with a grin.

"I can't believe you came all this way."

"I wouldn't miss this board meeting for anything in the world. And besides, I have a promise to make good on."

Just before David died, he had told Yvonne to call Thomas if ever she needed help. She'd seen Thomas at the funeral, where he had asked if she needed anything. No, she'd said, and for eighteen months, she hadn't bothered her husband's best friend for assistance, even though he'd called her from time to time to check in. But today, she was finally calling in a favor. Thomas had been installed as a board member of Christ-Life Sanctuary about ten years ago but rarely showed up for meetings. The board had always been in accord with David, so he'd never needed to rely on his friend for a tie-breaking vote.

Yvonne had no such luck, and so she'd asked for Thomas's help on this vote. Yet she hadn't expected him to make an appearance—not when he could have simply phoned in with his vote.

"Please, sit down," Yvonne said, gesturing to the couch. "Before we talk about church business, I want to know how you've been doing." It had been months since they'd caught up, and she was eager to hear about his speaking ministry and his family.

Thomas unbuttoned his suit jacket and sat down on the couch next to Yvonne. "So, what do you want to know?"

"For starters, you haven't been traveling as much lately. Has the world received all the motivation it needs?"

Thomas laughed. "I'm still getting more speaking engagements than I can accept, but I guess I've kind of lost my wanderlust."

Yvonne knew that for years, Brenda had asked Thomas to spend less time on the road and more time at home. It seemed strange that now, more than two years after Brenda's death, he was finally willing to limit his travels. "What brought this on?" she asked.

"Since Brenda died, I've spent a lot of time putting things into perspective. I want to spend some time reconnecting with my son, which is going to be hard since he has his own career now."

Yvonne understood exactly where Thomas was coming from. She and David had spent many years on the preaching circuit, and then, one day, they looked up and saw that Toya and Tia were grown. She wished she could take credit for the woman Toya had become, and she definitely wished that she had spent more time helping Tia mature. If life didn't turn out right for Tia, Yvonne knew she'd be tempted to blame herself. "I should have spent more time with my girls as they were growing up, too." She slapped her hand against her thigh as she sat up a bit straighter. "But, hey, I figure I'll get a second chance when they give me some grandchildren."

"Speak for yourself, Granny," Thomas said, nudging her arm. "I'm not trying to become a poppa for at least another five years. We didn't have Jarrod until I was thirty, so I figure he can at least return the favor and not have his first kid until he's at least thirty, maybe even thirty-five."

Yvonne chuckled, then laughed outright, so hard that she doubled over. When she finally regained composure, she sat up again and wiped the tears from her eyes. "Okay, maybe I don't want to be a granny so soon, either."

"You certainly don't look like any granny I know. I mean, look at you. You're fifty-two, but you don't look a day over forty."

Yvonne had been told that her looks were what Olay would want to advertise its facial products. Fifty was definitely the new forty where she was concerned. With her long, coal-black hair, light skin, and eyes that sparkled and danced, she could have passed for a relative of Lena Horne. "We've known each other entirely too long. There's no way you should know my real age."

Thomas lifted his hands in surrender. "Don't worry about it. I'll take your secrets to the grave with me."

"I don't want to hear anything about you going to your grave."

Thomas put an arm around Yvonne's shoulder and gave her a squeeze. "I shouldn't have said that. I'm sorry."

With his arm still wrapped around her, Yvonne took a deep breath to steady her nerves. She had seen two deaths too many in the past two years, and she didn't know if she could make it through funeral number three so soon. With David and Brenda gone, Yvonne felt that she should have fulfilled her quota of home-goings for a lifetime. "Don't say stuff like that. I don't consider it funny."

"Again, I'm sorry," Thomas said as he stood up. "Are you ready for the meeting tomorrow morning?"

Yvonne shook her head and leaned back in the couch. "I've been in ministry for thirty years, co-pastored Christ-Life for twenty, and now some board that my husband and I formed wants to vote me out. I don't know how to get ready for something like that."

"But I'm here to cast my vote in favor of you staying senior pastor of Christ-Life," Thomas reminded her. "And I believe several others will vote in your favor, also."

Yvonne pushed herself to her feet and planted a kiss on Thomas's cheek. "God love you for what you're doing, Thomas. But I don't know how much good it's going to do. If Deacon Brown has his way, I might need to take on a few of those speaking engagements you've cancelled."

"Don't worry," Thomas said. "This meeting is in the Lord's hands. He knows that you're meant to pastor this church, and I plan to do everything in my power to make the other board members realize that."

Order your copy of Our Love to continue reading…